VERY FEW PEOPLE
COME THIS WAY

Lyrical Episodes from
The Year of the Rabbit

Edward Seidensticker

In Print

In Print Publishing Ltd is registered with the Publishers Licensing Society in the UK and the Copyright Clearance Center in the USA.

British Library Cataloguing in Publication Data: a catalogue record for this book is available from the British Library.

ISBN 1 873 047 31 2

Cover design by Russell Townsend
Additional artwork by Zana Juppenlatz
Typeset by MC Typeset Ltd
Printed by Athenæum Press Ltd., Gateshead, Tyne & Wear.

First published in 1994 by
In Print Publishing, 9 Beaufort Terrace, Brighton BN2 2SU, UK.
Tel: (0273) 682836. Fax: (0273) 620958

About the author

Edward Seidensticker is at present Professor Emeritus of Japanese, Columbia University, New York. He is the English translator of Tanizaki Junichiro and Kawabata Yasunari and of *The Tale of Genji*. He is also the author of a history of Tokyo in two volumes, *Low City, High City* and *Tokyo Rising*.

But the longer I live in this Crumpetty Tree
The plainer than ever it seems to me
That very few people come this way. . . .
                    Edward Lear

I do not dissemble when I say:
Very few people come this way.
                    Shiraito Yoko

1. Miss Shiraito to Mr. Brown

A waning moon sheds light upon this garden in the western marches of Tokyo, and causes confusion. The night is a freezing one, as we enter the time of the Lesser Cold, beyond which lies the Greater; and there is this sluggish economy, and inflation. One must have reserves. I pray that yours are ample.

I must apologize for writing so early in the new year, which takes getting used to, without introduction. The coincidence of New Year's Day with a Day of Great Peace is so felicitous that it asks new beginnings. That is my excuse. Yet the affront to you, a guest of our land, is considerable.

Once I had an American intimate, but he went home. He too was a newspaperman, of New York. I feel that you will understand better, and stay longer.

Let me introduce myself. The second line on the reverse of the envelope is my name. The first element is the family name, the second the given. Can you surmise the gender of this second element? If not I will tell you, when we meet. It has reference to the sea. My father, who is in trade, was on one of his expeditions when I was born.

I am perhaps twenty-three years of age. I am a recent graduate of the White Lily Academy, where I took a major in English and one in botany, and minors in ornithology and in Latin and the successor languages. Upon my graduation, with the assistance of my father, I obtained employment with Craft, a company of traders doubtless known to you. The company building, House of Craft, stands very near what was once the front gate to the palace but is no more, and not far from the Foreign Correspondents Club, where, I am told, you pass the hours. Were you to come calling, you would find me at my post upon the fifteenth floor, where also is the president's office, steeping tea. I sometimes think of asking for more creative work, but ours is a narrow land, and our expectations must be trimmed. If done in a proper frame of mind, the steeping of tea is not entirely uncreative, especially here.

You will ask why I have chosen to become intimate with *you*, this propitious New Year's Day.

I inquired at the desk of the Foreign Correspondents Club for someone not likely to go the way of my other friend.

"Mr. Brown will be the last of them," said the young man. He was a sincere young man.

"Mr. Brown!" I said to myself.

Then there is your pithiness. No Japanese would have made the associations which you made, in the *Morning Flush* of the Sunday but two before last, between Mt. Fuji and those things.

"Mr. Brown!" I said to myself then too.

I will be hoping to hear from you.

This waning moon, coldly silver as it mounts into the sky, seems to make ironic comment upon the human condition.

> How happy, on its gibbous flight,
> To know where it may go,
> To know where it may sink!
> And what of me, this winter's night?
> I do not think I know.
> I do not know I think.

2. Miss Shiraito to Mr. Brown.

I choose a propitious day for continuing our correspondence, however briefly. It is a dark night. There is no moon. Upon the still, cold air, and in darkness as if to engulf it, there is a sweet scent, that of *Chimonanthus praecox*, "wax plum," say the dictionaries, not readily engulfed.

> Oh silly night!
> You try to hide
> It from my sight.
> My nose yet tells
> Whereat it dwells
> Because it smells.

I love *Chimonanthus praecox*, sending forth its sweet scent in the dark of night, as we enter the Lesser Cold, and, with determination and trumpery, prepare ourselves for the assaults of the Greater. I am sorry to say that my father brought back our original *Chimonanthus* from one of his marauding expeditions against the Chinese. I do not know whether he has been forgiven. I hope so.

I am inclined to think that my earlier note reached you. One of the small blessings for which we can we thankful in these narrow islands of ours is a postal system which continues, after a fashion, to function. The newspapers and weekly magazines keep telling us of mail sacks abandoned, in your own land, in vacant lots and lavatories. An explanation for our own small blessing may be a scarcity of these last.

I am somewhat grieved that I have had no answer. Your remarks in the *Morning Flush* about Tokyo smells make me feel confident that, were we together, we would be sharing this one. And it has been a wistful day in houses which, like that of the Shiraitos, adhere to feudal customs and manners in the taking down of New Year decorations.

> What had seemed vernal
> Once more is hibernal.

3

For out goes the greenness,
The holiday *Pinus*.

Might it be that you have doubts about my friendly intentions? Read the enclosed, if you will, and lay them at rest. It is
from the "Outcry" page of the *Morning Flush*, to which I am a
persistent contributor. You may not have noticed me as I have
noticed you, but the fact of our being together in the *Flush*
makes me think, somehow, that you are at the one end, and I at
the other, of a bond from a former life. Does it have that effect
upon you? This is my most recent contribution to "Outcry," and
the one best calculated, I think, to still your doubts.

I enclose as well my major unpublished *oeuvre* to date. It is
my White Lily graduation essay, "Was Eric Arthur Blair
(George Orwell) Aware That 1984 Will Be The First Year of
the Seventy-Ninth Sexagenary Cycle?" You will see that Dr.
Madder has remarked, at the end and at the beginning: "Pure
rubbish!" This is most probably a reference to my contribution
to "Outcry" on the subject of waste-free garbage disposal. Dr.
Madder is a puckish, abusive old English gentleman who has for
many years taught the Queen's English at White Lily.

I would like to tell you of my family, but midnight
approaches. It is a busy season. I sometimes think that we ring
out the old and ring in the new with altogether too much vigor.
Doubtless you too are busy. I look forward to hearing from
you, and to seeing you, after the dark of the moon has passed. I
hope that you have avoided the slippages and stoppages so
frequently induced by our New Year's food,

2a: The shorter enclosure to Miss Shiraito's letter

Some of My Best Friends are Americans
Shiraito Yoko
(Salaried person, Tokyo, Age 22)

It is a time for self-reflection. Another government has fallen.
Is this cause for cheering, and trumpery, and banners? No.

Another government has come in. Is the occasion one for felicitation? No.

"When we say 'imperialism is ferocious,' we mean that its nature will never change" (Chairman Mao).

This is the reason. It is a reason too frequently overlooked.

We have been administered opiates. We have been administered them in such quantities and over such expanses of time that we no longer know what the symptoms are. When one has fluctuations and calls a doctor, does one ask of him an opiate, that the discomfort, etc., may pass? No. Does one ask that he seek the sources? Yes.

Imperialists "will never become Buddhas, till their doom" (Chairman Mao). Therefore we need give voice to no huzzas when a new government comes.

I do not wish to be misunderstood. Some of my best friends are Americans. To them I do not weary of saying: "Let us be friends! Let us 'support whatever the enemy opposes and oppose whatever the enemy supports' (Chairman Mao)!"

3. Miss Shiraito to Mr. Brown

There was ice upon the pond when I arose, but it was broken by the variegated carp. Now, in languorous sunlight, it has melted quite away. How whimsical, beside the ice-coated pond, was the tiny little winter camellia. And what is this which I see here? I would have thought it too early for *Horeites diphone* and yet:

> Upon my garden path I ken –
> A fall of snow?
> Oh no! Ah no!
> A fall of damson petals then?
> Oh no! Ah no!
> Left by a warbler (or a wren)
> *Petits morceaux*!

It certainly was good that you came home before midnight. Very good it was that we are able to introduce ourselves, for a time. I was touched by your concern that I be on my way before the shops closed. And amused as well, for, you see, they were long since closed! I did as a matter of fact wander astray, but only once, briefly, down by the lake. I was able to attract the attention of a young lady and gentleman who were huddled together for warmth and inquire directions.

You are too modest when you refer to your lodgings as a hovel. I would not have thought that you had been in Japan long enough to learn such modesty, but then, of course, you are quick, and have a journalist's eye, ear, etc. In the matter of your garb, there may be a little in what you say.

I was so intent upon imbibing of your wisdom, and so entranced with your pithy American way of evincing it, especially upon Governor Minobe and upon sewage disposal (you did not always, I thought, keep the two ideally separated), that I did not tell you a fraction of the things you must know if we are to be friends.

I will tell you of my family.

We who gather for breakfast are five in number. I do not know that "gather" is the right word. Breakfast is the time when our comings and goings overlap, and a maximum attendance of five is likely, from time to time. There are my mother and father and myself. There is my brother, a recent graduate of a university which has no law school, which fact tells you all you need to know. He has thus far refused to let his time be occupied, save at the Cosa Nostra Pinball Parlor, where he passes his days. My sister is at White Lily, a member of a bund dedicated to rending the fabric. Actually I have one more of each, brother and sister, and it is to my younger older brother and my younger sister that I here refer. My older older brother lives out in the garden with his wife, who seems to make great demands upon his time. My older sister, also, is married, and lives in Sendai.

Sendai is my father's native place, and the legal residence for us all. My father seems to enjoy seeing it there, "Sendai," naked upon the family register, but to my Tokyo sensibilities it is like a proclivity. Sometimes at a White Lily reunion it is averred that I have a Sendai accent; and everyone laughs.

Let me introduce you to us as we were at breakfast this Sabbath morning, the overlap, for a time, complete.

"I do not know why I am keeping this great, childish newspaper from you children for whom it is intended," says my father, showing no inclination to pass it on to my brother, next in line. "You will be interested in the editorial. It tells us that we on the senile side of the gap have failed to provide adequate dreams for you on the juvenile. Taking always into account conditions and contingencies, it says, we must provide, for you, these last. Now how are we to go about it, I wonder. Yes, the *Flush* always has an answer to your questions. We are to talk things over. We are to arrange a series of interviews. Did you go for that interview yesterday?"

"I do not go for interviews. I did not. You know the former from experience, the latter from your detectives." The speaker is my brother. My father keeps arranging these interviews for him, with an eye to employment.

"Consult your busy schedule and mine, if you will, please, and tell me when the detectives could have found a time to report to me."

"They sometimes tie notes to the *Chimonanthus praecox*." It is I, seeking to inject a note of cheer.

"Is that book about the cuckoo's nest still on the lists?" It is my mother, seeking, no doubt, to do the same. In addition, she has this thing about cuckoos.

"We get best-seller lists Mondays. Sundays we get helpful household hints. Flushbudgets and the like. This morning we are advised in the matter of how to maintain our protein intake in the absence of soybeans, of which the Americans are about to deprive us."

"Without soybeans? Just think of it!"

"Without soybeans! How ever?"

"Peanut fabrications are recommended. It is going to be the Year of the Peanut. A richly goobernatorial year." Do you

7

know what a pivot word is? As our intimacy progresses and you become familiar with our great lyrical tradition and all its pivot words, you will come to see the cleverness (if I do say so myself) of my translation. "Are they talking about peanuts at Craft these days? If not they are delinquent."

"Yes," reply I, briefly.

"You must keep your ears, etc., open. You can learn, to the improvement of your English, what a variety of meanings the word 'peanut' has. Are you grateful that I got you there on top of Craft, where these opportunities are? No. Such numbers of things in this great daily of which White Lilies might learn with profit. There are fleas in the Vatican. How is that, for instance?"

But my sister, who believes in action and not words, is silent; and I am at the end of my tape.

Do you feel that you have got to know us a little?

If I may revert, for a moment, to my pivot word, they *do* these days discuss peanuts, in English, at House of Craft, and I do not always quite understand the meaning. It is a matter which I hope we may put on our agenda.

And I hope that you are on your guard against malign influences from Hong Kong and Korea. It is among the seasons for them.

4. Mr. Brown to Miss Shiraito

Thank you very much indeed for the almanac. Though informing me that today is Adults' Day, it raises as many questions as it answers.

> Oh I am one, and are you too?
> And if you are, then tell me, do,
>   How best to register my exultation.
> For ours it is, this joyous day,

And ours the need to find a way
    To manifest in full the adult station.
So bang the timbrels, whang the timbals,
    As we show our adult symbols.

Or am I wrong?

I enjoyed my time in House of Craft yesterday. At first I feared I had made a mistake in asking the security guard for directions. He drew me several maps, and all I really needed to know was the way to the elevator. I emerged presently from this, and there you were, steeping tea. You too were very kind. I like the sumptuous quiet of your library, and think that I will go there often, to read the *Wall Street Journal*.

On my way out I asked another question and had a pleasant hour looking around while he prepared the answer.

I watched the Koreans get frisked. That was fun.

I have argued that there is no way to tell a Korean from a Japanese. I see now that there is.

You erect a security barrier, and you say to him who approaches, if you have reason to suspect: "And might your honorable person be of the Land of Han?"

If he replies, "Even so," you frisk him.

You must of course be on guard against the prevarication in which these people indulge. "You will excuse me, I am sure, and not think it the thing of my not believing you," you say, when something, a whiff of garlic, perhaps, has alerted you to the improbability that he is of the Land of Yamato; and you frisk him.

Nothing in the least suspicious emerged from the pocket or briefcase of a single child of Han, of whom there must have been a dozen while I waited; and my own blue-eyed kind was scarcely inspected at all.

There was an exception.

A child of Han made protest: "And why have you not looked into the large, suspicious Boston bag of him of the Western Sea?"

It was true. A large New York type was even then heading

9

for the elevator. He had a large black bag, which I would not myself have described as a Boston one, but that is all right. The guard had to stop him, of course. Gazing at the ceiling mirror and whistling a tune, I saw that the bag contained neat packets the size of bank notes.

"A primitive banking system," he said, looking up with a large New York grin and catching my eye in the ceiling mirror.

"It would never work if this were a city of muggings."

"You can say that again." And he went his way, not further detained. The child of Han was still being frisked.

I think that, in a general way, I know the answers to some of the fascinating questions suggested by this little pantomime.

> Sing a song of sixpence,
>   Packets full of dough,
> Infundibulation
>   To and not so fro.
> Is there, re the peanuts
>   Passing with the flow,
> Predetermination?
>   Yes and not so no.

Who is this New York person, whom you have probably seen? He looks like a dark, shaggy Boston bag himself. He went to one of the top floors, very possibly your own fifteenth. Where is it he lives, and what is it he does? What does he do by day, and what does he do by night? We must indeed put "peanuts" on our agenda. English too has pivot words.

You have just telephoned. That was kind of you. I will mail this letter all the same. Your complaint about the busy signal is well taken. There is a flurry of interest in the new government, and there are calls about this and that item for the morning paper. It was a nice long talk we had, was it not?

I am taking your advice and bundling myself securely against influences from Hong Kong and Korea.

5. Miss Shiraito to Mr. Brown

Such a lovely fall of snow as we did have in the night! And now it is so cold, so clear, so majestic, with no moon in the sky, and the snow as if brightly refulgent. I would have liked to stay up all night admiring it, and take the day off; but with our limited resources we cannot permit ourselves such fobbles.

I can see the question forming itself upon your practical American lips: "Well why the hell doesn't she just *take* the day off, if the snow is all that important to her?" This last is quite as you say. Yet I cannot. It will be a day of weddings, and I must keep the kettle boiling.

Why, you ask further, will it be a day of weddings? Consult your almanac for an answer.

"Superstition." I see the word forming itself upon those American lips. This, too, is true; but one is what one is.

And now the day breaks, and how very blue the sky is, and how white the snow. There are kites in the sky, of the kind attached to little boys, and of the free, feathered kind, *Milvus migrans lineatus*. I quite gasp at the beauty of the latter, and always have, in the clear, cold air.

> All I can say is oh! and oh!
> At (oh!) this morning's fall of snow.
> And oh! and oh! and my! and my!
> At *Milvi* (oh my!) milling by,
> At gledes a-gliding through the sky.

I too dislike telephoned trivia. A dislike for them runs in the family. My grandmother in Sendai announced when she turned sixty that she was not going to answer the telephone again for the rest of her life. Growing old must have its reasons, she said, for why else would it be?

My father has said that he is going to do the same when he reaches sixty. His sixtieth birthday is not far off, and he has already commenced turning away telephone calls by pretending to be deaf. The other morning we could all hear the gentleman next door shouting into the telephone his complaints about the mynah bird, and my father pretending to be incapable of catching them over the telephone. How we all did laugh, and the mynah bird the loudest!

Anyway, I share your dislike for telephones. Have you had the calls traced? Have you thought of hiring a detective? Does the voice suggest a lady, or a gentleman, or a Japanese?

I wished to get started with my letter while the world was clean and still, and the urge was upon me. It is now later in the morning, and I have been to breakfast.

My sister came in wearing a crash helmet. Would you like to go and look at the barricades? Take along a crash helmet of your own, if you do, making sure, to avoid police harassment, that it is of none of the usual student colors, black, white, red, violet, indigo, blue, green, yellow, orange, beige, and ecru.

"Excellent," said my father, taking up the *Morning Flush*. "I always did think that you would be better in the fire department, or on a construction site."

"I will be away for a time," came my sister's voice hollowly from the recesses of the helmet.

"Must it be so?" said my mother. "Should you not tell her not to?"

"Do not."

"I will."

"See?"

"What shall I tell people who telephone?"

"That there comes a time."

"Tell them that she is too young to answer the telephone. That will give them something to think about. And see who now joins us. A person from the flood brigade, to make us feel doubly protected, fire brigade and flood. But surely on this lucky day we need not be quite so protected?"

My brother had come in, a towel wrapped around his Afro. My father's water image was not as exaggerated as it might seem. When my brother washes his Afro, it drips every which way. I do not know why he washes it before breakfast on lucky days, unless he thinks that we might stop noticing.

"Are you going to tell me to tell him not to?"

But my mother had already started for the garden.

"If I could only turn them around," said my father, as if to the *Morning Flush.* "Him for her, and vice versa, sending him forth to do battle with the unrighteous, and keeping her at home with her hair endlessly drying. And what would I do, you ask, if I had to choose the one or the other? Why then I would send them both forth to do battle. Here is the new minister of education, taking on the teachers' union. Does he not know that it will still be here, unchanged, long after he is gone? So it is too with the unrighteous, though I do hope that the fight will be a good one. What did you wash your hair in, that it should give off that offensive odor? It puts me in mind of what that young American reporter said about our governor."

So you see you have an audience.

You have indicated such a warm interest in my family, about which I prefer not to talk. I do not worry about my sister. She will be gone for a time, and we will have the animating sight of barricades from the administration building along past Holy Jesus, and that will be fine. I do worry about my brother. His days at the Cosa Nostra Pinball Parlor are not without gain, for he brings home the cigarettes and chocolate bars that are the premiums for fine play. This is not, however, enough to satisfy my father. In my father's voice this morning there was an especial snap. It may have been directed at Governor Minobe, but he usually does not think Governor Minobe worth a snap. I may wish to ask your advice, about my brother, actually my half-brother. We were reared almost as twins, our ages similar as it is possible, in the case of full siblings, only for the ages of twins to be.

My sister straightened her helmet, and my brother took off his towel, revealing a real diller of an Afro, and our breakfast was at an end.

"You are looking very ladylike this morning," said my father to me. I left without a word.

It is yet later in the morning. Preparatory to making my way on foot to the station, there to take the first of several trains for the city, I caught a few winks. I must tell you of a complex dream I had. "Why, here I am dreaming of Mr. Brown," said I to myself in the dream, knowing that it was a dream, which, I think, makes it a duplex dream, or more. Of such a dream, many poets of old would have said:

> Within a dream, I dreamed of you,
> Which makes a count of two.
> And had the choice been mine to make
> (And be my count quite true)
> I would have wished to go on dreaming
> Twice (my count) of you.

So they would have said, all those poets of old.

Preparatory to mailing this letter, from the heart of the city, at which I have by stages now arrived, I have sought several times to telephone, and each time received the busy signal. Are you being bothered again? I keep thinking your apartment needs something, maybe a citrus tree. Would you like a *Citrus tachibana*?

Do take care of yourself in this time of mounting cold. I must work tomorrow, for Craft does not take the modern view of Saturdays; but I will be free on Sunday, and at your beck.

6. Mr. Brown to Miss Shiraito

We have entered the Greater Cold, I am informed, by a lady who keeps entering my rooms in hot pursuit of cockroaches. The moon is fuller every night. I offer felicitations and exhortations.

Thank you very kindly for the citrus tree. The watchman expressed great surprise when I told him of it. He remembered you, but not it. I may tell you that a fellow would not come home late at night in New York and find a strange citrus tree upon his desk.

It surprises me that you should keep getting the busy signal.

The probabilities are low. Were the Pope or Chairman Mao to keep getting it I would not be so surprised.

I will be hoping to see you. I have a lady friend, American, who is living in Kyoto and will be spending a few days in Tokyo next week. She is on the faculty of an American university, and she is studying discontented women. In particular she is studying a femininist organization called the Choopy Wren, with which I had not been familiar until she described it to me.

> The Choopy Wren, the Choopy Wren.
> Oh say it again, do say it again!
> Very well, just once: the Choopy Wren.

She will be staying at Cosmopolitan Culture House. Perhaps we could arrange to meet there, or at the Press Club. We could meet here, only I have a feeling that the citrus tree does not like callers. If you can introduce my friend Hilda, for Hilda Gray is her name, to some discontented women, we will both be most grateful.

We twit each other, Hilda Gray and I, about Kyoto and Tokyo.

"There may be other cities in the world that teem in larger measure than Tokyo with discontented women, but there are none in Japan. And why am I not then in Tokyo studying them?"

". . .?"

"Because at heart I will always be a Pekingese."

". . .?"

"This is the nearest we will ever get to it again. I mean *that* is. I forget where I am, sometimes."

"The two cannot be all that different, if you forget. But they are."

"But they are."

"The one is far from as good as it thinks it is, and the other is far better than it thinks it is."

"And which is the one, and which the other?"

"Kyoto is the one, and Tokyo the other."

"I think you are right. But maybe the one *ought* to have a

superiority, and the other an inferiority, complex."

"Kyoto is merely dull and pompous."

"Tokyo is merely vulgar."

So we go on amiably twitting and chiding each other. You may have guessed that Miss Hilda Gray's cultural origins are Chinese. Throw her a Chairman Mao, and she will throw one right back at you. Yet I must warn you that she is not one of those unconditional idolaters. Not long ago she was remarking on how very Chinese it is of them to have the calendar begin at 2697 B.C. Why could they not, she said, have been sensible people and chosen a round figure?

I sometimes feel that the Greater Cold is coming at me over the telephone wires. And there it is, my citrus tree, all through the long winter night, growing.

7. Miss Shiraito to Mr. Brown

Most things this evening are next to perfect for letters. You may have observed the fall of snow earlier in the day. Now a full moon has come out, the only full moon we will have in this time of the Greater Cold.

> All out of sight,
> The *Prunus* white,
> This moonlit night.
> My nose can tell
> Where it doth dwell
> Yet by the smell.

If the night is one of moonlight, you are asking, in that practical American way, why then is the *Prunus* white all out of sight? Because silver predominates. A Japanese would have known immediately.

It is a potted plum. I look at it, and I think of you looking at your *Citrus tachibana*, also potted, and it is as if there were

16

something. Do you not agree? I was very glad to have your letter, and even gladder to come upon your person, in the Press Club. The lunch was among the more pleasurable ones in recent memory. When I got back to the office, all rosy with beer and hotchpotch, the other girls tittered and pointed and tittered. I said that I had been to a *miai* ("a marriage meeting": Kenkyusha's Japanese-English Dictionary, third edition, page 1094), which silenced them.

"Whose *miai* was it? Yours, in part?" said Mr. Minawata, the president's secretary. He was on his way to the gentlemen's room, or rather, the gentlemen's door. He took the ladies' door, by mistake, I should imagine. There is a ladies' door and there is a gentlemen's, and once inside it is all the same.

I looked rosily downwards. Such a silence, you could have cut it.

"Marrying money, I hope," said he, emerging yet another time from the ladies' door.

"'If the shoe fits,'" said I, quoting.

I doubt that I had ever before been the recipient of such a silence.

Since you have shown such a warm interest in my family, let me introduce you briefly to a weekday breakfast. My sister is absent from our breakfast scene. She has been absent since the Sabbath breakfast to which I introduced you in my fourth letter. My mother is down in the garden, gathering creatures for the mynah bird. So the count of five is reduced to three, my father, my younger older brother, and myself.

My father speaks, the *Morning Flush* before him, open at the "Outcry" page.

"That Shiraito Yoko is at it again. She burns, it seems, with anger. Either she has had a birthday, or she does not know how old she is. Or maybe she moves back and forth between the new system and the old, thereby giving symbolic expression to the agony of the modern Japanese intellectual. Did you go for the interview yesterday?"

He has a way of abruptly changing the object of his address, as if confident that heed is being paid. For your information and whatever action you may wish to take, I enclose my most recent publication, to which reference has just been made.

"Why do you always ask," says my brother, "when you have other and more reliable sources of information?"

"Because I wish to be civil. What was your reason for not going?"

"I was busy, having other things to do. It was not a good day."

"It was a very good day. That is why I chose it."

"I was busy, having other things to do."

"Soon it will be spring." Thus do I seek to change the subject, cheerfully.

"If I believed you," says my father, consigning my effort to ears as if deaf, "I would say to myself: why here is news."

"You know what I was doing. Belief and disbelief have nothing to do with the matter."

"You think, do you, that I think you worth the trouble and expense of having trailed?"

"Of having trailed? They do it whether you ask them or not. They must enjoy it."

"Whether they do or whether they do not, it is not from them that I have my information. It is from *her*, rather. I am not unable, when I try, to put two and two together; and the suddenly constricted flow of chocolate bars and cigarettes into this house led me to make inquiry of her as to whether she might know the reason. She did, or at least she has a persuasive theory. This is the information which I have at my disposal. Bear in mind, as you lay plans for having no future, that I am sufficiently interested in the matter to put two and two together."

With that my father takes up a raw egg, more silent than usual. It is thus for the rest of the meal, and my brother behaves as if the silence were his own precious handiwork, under no circumstances to be broken. My brother departs the house immediately after breakfast.

Again I have a reason other than the warm interest you have always expressed in the affairs of my family for bringing you to our breakfast table. Might your sources of information be such as to reveal to you who "her" might be, the "her" upon whom my father placed such peculiar emphasis? For it was peculiar.

I look forward most eagerly to meeting your Professor Gray. For her sake, I have taken membership in the main (Tokyo) chapter of the Chupiren. Were you to ask me: are you, Ms. Shiraito, in sympathy with the immediate goals of the Chupiren, its advocacy of abortion (*chu*) and the pill (*pi*) – were you thus to make query of me, I would have to reply: it is not the specifics, Mr. Brown, but the spirit. To this last the enclosure indirectly addresses itself. Please do not read into it anything personal. As to whether or not your Professor Gray will find in our main (Tokyo) Chupiren the sort of discontented woman she is looking for, well, you know the pastoral American proverb about the horse and the water, not that I would wish to liken her, whom I have not met, to a horse, or them to water.

The moon has climbed to and past zenith, and here is beginning another new day. It is the Day of the Chicken. And here already is chanticleer, as if claiming his own, In a few hours all of us economic animals will be rushing in upon this pure cleanness, doing to it what we have just done to the Straits of Malacca, for which I apologize. I like to think of you viewing it as well, you through your potted *Citrus tachibana*, I through my plum, also potted. But the image of you tucked in all snugly in bed is, as well, pleasing.

7a: The enclosure to Miss Shiraito's letter

We Burn with Anger

Shiraito Yoko
(Salaried Person, Tokyo, Age 23)

I have followed your correspondence upon the commencement of International Women's Year with very great interest, and with awe and quavering, as well, at the magnitude of the problems before us.

And there is also, alas, it must be said, anger!

In regard to this last, I must address myself particularly to Mr. Akahata (Organization Functionary, Age 48), whose contribution to "Outcry" appears in yours of the twenty-third inst.

Mr. Akahata: if not even intellectuals understand, how are the prospects? Unpromising.

Yes, Mr. Akahata, it is true that among Chairman Mao's injunctions to the Red Army is this one: "(7) Do not take liberties with women." Yet to change this, as you suggest to: "(7) To not take liberties with persons" – this is to demonstrate (and you an organization functionary!) a deplorably inadequate grasp of the theory of contradictions.

My indignation rises, quavers. If this is what we may expect from organization functionaries, what then may we expect that it is in them to expect of us? Nothing.

Do they think that we are mindless beasts? Yes. The anger that is pent up in me, and countless others like me, will one day burst forth, to write a new page in Japanese history, and International Women's Year.

We burn with anger.

8. Miss Gray to Mr. Brown

You were very kind, and I enjoyed my time in Tokyo. You demand of me nasty remarks about Tokyo, that the running battle which has been at the heart of our friendship may continue, and I would be as regretful as you to see it go. Yet I may say that anyone who would be bored in Tokyo would be bored while trying to outswim a shark. My landlady argues, however, that Kyoto is where the old money is.

You are right to laugh about my Choopy Wrens. I laugh too. I think of myself as a liberal scholar, and the essence of liberal scholarship is the pursuit of the useless with intense dedication.

Miss Shiraito was very kind in introducing me to Choopy Wrens. I had brought introductions with me from Kyoto, but in this as in so many things there is factionalism, a Tokyo Choopy preferring an anti-Choopy of the most virulent kind to a Kyoto Choopy. It was far better to be escorted by a paid-up Tokyo member. If you can tactfully learn how much it cost her to get paid up, I will certainly wish to reimburse her.

The meeting was highly confessional. Members were encouraged to stand and tell how they kicked the habit. To suggestions that she do so, Miss Shiraito responded with brief statements ending in "but."

"It is not that I do not wish to speak, but."

"My own experience is so very limited, but."

"I would not wish to have it thought that I would wish to have it thought otherwise, but."

There was an exchange between Miss Kurozora, the president, and me.

"It is good that you have an American friend, Shiraito. It is good, I say, for we have so much to learn from the right kind of American. I am sure that everything you have heard tonight, Gray, must strike you as pale and puny when measured against your own experience."

"I might have a thing or two to tell you, back on my own stamping ground." I think it important to project an American image.

"This statement informs you what you must do, Shiraito. There is so much to be learned from the land of tough, unyielding womanhood, a land where one cannot, it is said, tell the sexes apart, except by – do not be parsimonious with your knowledge, Gray. I am sure that we will wish to borrow some of your devices."

"Likewise."

"I descend to Kyoto from time to time. I find that I tend to feel more welcome at abodes of alien persons than at those of Kyoto persons, who have acquired the notion that they are in the forefront. This I need not tell you. You have had intercourse with our Kyoto branch, I believe."

"We have exchanged howdydos."

"You must tell me about their good points. Doubtless you

have come upon some. And you, Shiraito? Do you ever descend to Kyoto?"

"Yes, but. No, but."

"Yes, Gray, indeed you must. I wonder if the eleventh of next month might be convenient. My schedule should permit a descent to your part of the country on that day."

"It's my birthday. Get yourself up, Miss Shiraito, and haul yourself down for a bash."

"No, but."

"Just fancy. Such a day to have selected for your birthday, and an American too – let me just write that down and have someone – do you have a few spare bedrooms? Those Kyoto people always put me next to the men's room. However often I tell them, they *will* put me – do you have reason or have you ever had reason to suspect that the C.I.A. had something to do with the selection of your birthday?"

Have you? I have not forgotten that it is coming, this birthday which we share, you and I, with the nation.

Thank you again for your kindness, and thank you too for the clippings, and especially your article about the new minister of education. Do you really think that he will make a difference? How many dozens of ministers of education have there been, I wonder, since the commencement of the MacArthur Enlightenment, and which of them has made a whit of difference? In this regard my views accord with those of Miss Shiraito's father, as she has passed them on to me.

> Eyes right, O minister of education,
> And left, you educators of the nation,
> And we, our gaze now dexter and now sinister,
> Will watch the education of the minister.

Kyoto is very cold, colder than Tokyo. These dark rooms which the sun never visits, not because it is cut off by other rooms or buildings but because it is not welcome – even in such *The Tale of Genji* was written, all through the enormous length of which there is no mention of chilblains. I cannot think why.

Perhaps there was no need to mention them because everyone had them. They could be assumed.

9. Miss Shiraito to Miss Gray

Despite the harsh dryness of the winds that blow down upon us from western regions, spring has come next door (as the poets say).

> Just enough light from the wintertime sun
> For blossom of *Prunus mume* one.

It puts forth its one blossom in a sunny southern corner of a veranda, and I honor it with a time-honored haiku, which I have revised to conform to the findings of modern botany. Warmth has nothing to do with the blooming *Prunus*. It is light, rather, the lengthening of the days.

I did enjoy sitting with you and Mr. Brown in a sunny corner of Cosmopolitan Culture House, surrounded by its types. On and on, I would have wished to listen to them, your opinions on many subjects, and Mr. Brown's. I have however gone over my tapes several times since your departure, and, borrowing from the wisdom of Chairman Mao Tse-tung, I think that I must venture a demurrer. "On a blank piece of paper free from any mark the freshest and most beautiful characters can be written, the freshest and most beautiful pictures can be painted." Had you thought of *that*?

I hope that you did not take back to Kyoto with you a feeling that the discontented womanhood of the city might be more to your purpose. Let me, aqainst that possibility, tell you what happened this afternoon.

I became aware something was different when Mr. Minawata asked me to deliver a message to the teacher of flower arranging of the president, Mr. Kuromaku, whose private secretary and executive assistant Mr. Minawata is.

23

"Tell her of the Little Old School whom you will find out upon the terrace," said Mr. Minawata, "that the president has contracted a mild something and cannot see her today."

I knew that it was not true. I had just taken tea to Mr. Kuromaku, who was his usual evocative self, in conference with the president of Turbulines, our second largest airline, in the matter of the American airplanes that will be necessary if a stranglehold is to be obtained on Waikiki.

"But why not she of the Aobanas?"

I knew that out on the terrace I would find the grandest arranger of them all, of the Little Old School of Flower Arranging. It should have been Ms. Aobana's duty to go out and beard her, for it is she who has been assigned to mastering the vocabulary which these delicate missions ask. Her politeness, when the occasion is right, can be murderous. I wished that she had chosen another day for her demonstration, which is what proved to obtain.

"She is not to be seen," said Mr. Minawata, "this Thursday afternoon."

She *had* been – and there she was, reading one of those do-it-yourself manuals on frangible grenades. But she was not in uniform! She had stripped!

Now we Crafteuses, as our *haute couturiere* calls us, are required to wear uniforms. The men are not. It is true that they might as well be, for all the variety that is to be discerned in their garb, but that is another matter. They are as alike as the peanuts which Mr. Kuromaku and he of Turbulines were discussing each time I went in to refill their teacups.

"I will send around someone of secretarial rank," said the Grand Arranger, thereby putting me in my place, "to make inquiry as to when I am expected again, and to give, in return, apprehension as to whether or not the expectation is realistic." She left behind on the terrace an ingenious assortment of belaboring devices, doubtless for the secretarial type to pick up.

Like everyone else, I allowed an opaque shutter to descend between me and Ms. Aobana. What else is a person to do, in these circumstances? And then, for a time, we returned to normalcy. She was once again in uniform, the company emblem, a palm outstretched as if for a purpose, upon her bosom.

And then beside me once again was Mr. Minawata.

"The president wishes his (good) lady to be told, by telephone or other expeditious means, to unpack."

I knew without looking down the rows of desks that Ms. Aobana would have stripped once more.

This mission too was cause for trepidation. Once more I was put in my place.

"I cannot begin to express my thanks," said Ms. Kuromaku, over the telephone, which means of communication I bravely chose, though a courier would have been possible, "at your so cheerfully acquitting yourself of duties for which none of your previous experience, when you came in off the streets to join us, can have prepared you."

She was angry. She knows very well that I obtained my position because her husband and my father were together in Tokyo University and, earlier, in a Sendai high school. She had planned to go to Waikiki for the weekend, but apparently the Turbulines discussions had rendered it impolitic that she do so. So it is with strangleholds. Someone is always inconvenienced.

Our afternoon passed, thus. Ms. Aobana would be for a time back in uniform, and the Craft spirit would prevail, "All for Craft and Craft for all." I would be sent on no difficult missions. And then it would happen again.

You Americans are always saying that to strip once serves quite as well as to do it ten times, but you are wrong.

Just a lunar month ago, on this same Nineteenth Night, my intercourse with Mr. Brown began. It has been productive of so many things, among them my friendship with you, Professor Hilda Gray. The moon now rises over the garden of my eastern neighbor, a wealthy manufacturer of masticatories thought to be Korean. In my mind's eye I see you in your ancient capital observing it as well. But stay; you are four or five degrees, or sixteen or twenty minutes, farther to the west, and then there are those hills.

Sing hey and nonny-no, and sing high-oh to
All you who lie up later in Kioto.
For mountains all about you long have stood,
And there is likewise too the longitude.

When may Tokyo hope to see you again? Though we advance nearer to spring, you must not let yourself be cajoled into a lowering of your defenses.

10. Mr. Brown to Miss Gray

Thank you for your letter, and thank you for coming to see us. You are very good-natured about Tokyo. Your remarks hit the bull's eye, as we say in that pastoral way of ours. I become very impatient with people who tell me that Tokyo is an ugly city. They miss the point. It is an ugly city; but one can be fond of an ugly face, and one can come to loathe a beautiful face.

I conveyed your message to Miss Shiraito when she came calling last evening. She says that you must not think of seeking to repay her. She says that her one concern is lest the demurrer which she registered in her recent letter (she did not tell me what it was) have been too harsh. I find her interesting, and such an amusing blend of Mao and Eisenhower, and so full of information, too, which she scarcely seems to know she has. She sat a considerable spell, giving forth with pulings (her word for them) on a number of subjects. The moon presently rose over the garden of my eastern neighbor, whom she suspects of being Korean, and she commented upon it at length.

She did not tell me of certain happenings high in Craft of which she told you, she says, in her most recent letter. We are so close, she said, the three of us, that what is hers is mine and yours, and what is yours is mine and hers, and what is mine is yours and hers, etc. Therefore she did not tell me.

"Alike," she said dreamily, "as peanuts in a pod," referring to the habits of dress of the men of Craft. "As I was saying to Professor Gray, in a recent letter, written under the Moon of the Nineteenth Night."

Now "peanuts" is a pivot word which we have between us, and I become all ears when it is spoken. In the Craft context is it especially fascinating.

"Which comes first, I wonder," she said, "the peanuts or the airplanes? It was not clear."

The night had meanwhile drawn on.

"And now it is the Sabbath,"

"So soon," said I.

"That they may rest from their labours," said she then. "Revelation 14, 13."

It is called International Cultural Exchange. She is far better at it than I am.

I hope that we will see you in Tokyo again soon. The weather has been lovely. The *Prunus mume* in the shrine below me are coming into bud, dots of white against dark boughs. *Daphne odora* comes into bud as well, and soon will be odorous all over. But do remember that it is still winter.

> The harsher winter voice yet ling-
> Ers on for all these notes of spring.

11. Miss Shiraito to Mr. Brown

Oh happy day! Spring came in at thirty-five minutes past seven in the evening, by the solar reckoning. By the lunar it will not arrive until next month and someone's birthday, either yours or Professor Gray's, I forget which. I seem to gave left my memorandum book and the pertinent tapes somewhere.

> And here, before the year is over, why't
> Is spring! And what shall old, what new, be hight?

It is a translation. Spring has come by the solar calendar, that is what the poet is saying; but by the lunar, *au contraire*, the old year has not yet worked itself out. I do not doubt that these matters are puzzling to you foreigners.

You have asked whether your grapefruit should be pruned. Dr. Madder thinks not. He knows about these things. As a defense against the thorns, he recommends rocks. My mother is always bringing them home from rubble fairs. I might pass a few on.

It is kind of you to be interested in my family. I think of myself as a private person, not given to shouting from rooftops. Yet I must admit to a certain pleasure in responding to a demand, in this regard, when I become aware of one.

As at the breakfast of which I informed you in my last letter, now upwards of a week ago, my brother was present at breakfast this morning.

"Did you go for the interview yesterday?" my father asked.

"I was busy, having other things to do," said my brother. "It was not a good day."

"I knew that it was not a good day. I knew also that this fact would make no practical difference, and I wanted you to know that I knew. The good weather is about to end."

He said no more. It took him no longer than usual to see that there was nothing of interest on the front page of the *Flush* (is it so too with American newspapers?), and he departed without a glance at the several other pages.

"I have been seeing her," said my brother, *sotto voce*.

The house was quiet. My mother was gorging the mynah bird.

"Who is her?"

"The her who figured in the last remarks we had from the honorable mouth of our father at the last breakfast we shared."

"You have taken long enough, this being the case, in telling me."

"I do not like bombshells. You must go to another member of the family for them. I like adequate preparation and adequate warning. I prefer the rattlesnake to the lynx, the noisy American to the quiet one. Which is your Mr. Brown?"

You are becoming a friend of the family.

"Who *is* her?"

"Mother."

"You see her most of the days of your life. If you have not seen her this morning, it is only because there is something about you. She notices."

"You know what I mean."

I did, of course. He meant his real mother. You will remember from my fourth letter, not counting the enclosure to my second, that my younger older brother is really my half-brother. We do not have a mother in common.

"And how did you find her?"

"The policeman in the box knew more about her than it was necessary, in the line of his duties, that he know."

"You know what I mean."

"Her kimono was a knotted pattern of hemp leaves against a burnt-amber ground, and her obi, of antique violet, was decorated with *Prunus mume*, perhaps a quarter or a third of the way into bloom."

"But what did she *look* like?"

"You know what I mean."

I did. He had painted a word picture of a middleaged lady sufficiently handsome to be set off advantageously by expensive but unassertive modes of traditional dress. I would not wish to be understood as suggesting that, in our ill-endowed part of the world, integuments are held to make the person. Yet it may be that we are more of the view than are you that evidences of spirit are to be detected in attention to surfaces.

"And how was it that you came upon her? Not by accident, I suppose?"

"I went to see her after she had come to me. I have described her as she appeared in the Cosa Nostra Pinball Parlor, not by accident, I believe. Since then, I have several times been to see her, and indeed she has asked me to stay with her. She keeps a tea house over beyond the river."

I must, at this point, tell you a thing or two about Japanese

29

adoption practices. In some ways we in our cramped insular society may, I think, flatter ourselves upon being more open than you in your expansive continental society. It is the usual thing for a parent to know the whereabouts of a child put out for adoption, which in any event means no more than modifying the biological facts for purposes of registration. I doubt that there ever was an attempt to keep my brother's whereabouts from his real mother, nor would there have been ways of keeping her in ignorance had the intent been present. It may be somewhat more difficult, but I doubt that it is often impossible, for a foster child to learn the identity and whereabouts of his or her real parents. If I were a natural parent, I think I would prefer our way to yours. And if I were a natural child – I do not know. I shall observe my brother's behavior, and it may be that I shall presently have a view of the matter which you may wish to pass on to the people of Los Angeles.

"Does Father know?"

"Of course. He has his detectives, and they have to have something to keep them busy. You mean does he know that she has asked me to stay with her? Probably. She is an open sort, and at least as far as she is concerned he seems a persuasive sort."

I did not ask whether Mother knew. She just then came through on her way to the garden, looking like a fireperson.

"Is she married?"

"She has been. The tearoom is nicely done. The woodwork is good and not imported, and the girls wear kimono, and not the zip-on kind. I have not asked where she got the money."

"Do. Do!"

"I am sure that Father could tell you."

"Maybe I could go with you some time. But I think I doubt it would be a good idea."

"I think I do too."

Mother came back through. She had some things in spider webs for the mynah bird. Integuments do not always – I would not argue that they do – tell us much about the person beneath, and her expansive garden togs certainly told us very little. Yet there were in the lines and the flow certain hints that her absence from the breakfast table, upon which everything had been laid out to cool, was not fortuitous. The maid had looked in a couple of times, as if to make sure that nothing was getting hot.

I sense a crisis in my brother's affairs. To me the most important little detail in the conversation I have just transcribed for you is his reference to my father as "a persuasive sort." And my father said: "The good weather is about to end."

I trust that you do not destroy my letters, for there is a continuity in them. Are you taking to heart my advice about tapes? I hope so. It is good advice.

This first night of solar spring is a very dark one. Stars are returning to our Tokyo skies, even as little fishes to the River Sumida. We have not made much of stars in our great lyrical tradition. Ours is a moony literature. About the only stellar thing which it contains is an image borrowed from China, signifying an assignation as brief as the separation which follows is long. I hope that it will not be so with us.

> Although we be far as the far-distant clouds,
> 'Twill not be so always. No more of these doubts!
> The moon courses forth (even when in eclipse),
> And it comes back again. Of the round kind its trip's!

Do not let anyone tell you that the advent of spring means the utter departure of cold. I hope that you are amply tucked in, proclivities and all.

12. Miss Shiraito to Miss Gray

Is it with you as it is with us? With us, what was once among the busiest times of the year is now among the quietest. Just at this season, under the old calendar, we would all have been pounding glutinous rice and things, and paying bills and making calls, and decorating our gates with the festive *Pinus*. Under the new calendar, all that is over. Very few people come this way. It is one of the things which Commodore Matthew Calbraith Perry, U.S.N., did to us. (Did he do anything to anyone else?) In a sheltered corner against my father's study, which pushes southward from the house and has more sun than any other room, *Daphne odora* is about to open. *Daphne odora* is one of several flowers that are best when blown but a fraction. When it is blown in full, why then I think even you Americans must notice. It is cruelly oppressive of the more delicately scented *Prunus mume*, and yet I am not sure that I do not like it the better of the two, being taken back to the days of all days for wee girls, those quiet days when, all thumbs, we made ready for the Doll Festival.

> I shouldn't, I know, but there you have me,
> Admiring the plum less than Smelly Daphne!

A second poem is forming itself in my mind. Let it form, as I tell you of other things.

I will tell you of my younger sister, with whom I shared those days.

I visited White Lily recently, the occasion being the fortnightly reunion of my graduating class. There they were, not unexpected: barricades.

Past them I had to make my way to the site of the reunion. They were garrisoned by persons all helmets and tea towels above and all denim below. Voices, feminine, were raised in double *Sprechchor*, antiphonal.

"Pulverize/Sister Blanche." So went the antiphonal *Spechchor*. "Pulverize/Sister Blanche."

Impetuous young persons, wishing always to pulverize one another, or someone, or something! Their sincerity communicates itself.

Now Sister Blanche is the chief flower in the White Lily garland, the Superior. Oleofication might be a better word than pulverization, for she is corpulent. She is also French, and it does not seem at all hospitable for young persons to urge pulverization of a guest of our island land. Yet their sincerity does communicate itself, and is only with very great difficulty denied.

I thought I detected a familiar wail, in among the chanting. I made towards it. Staves were brandished at me as I did so, but I was undaunted – for what is democracy about?

"Why don't you stop by the house now and then? You could do it when Father is not around. He does not care a fig what you do, provided you get married some time and he does not see your picture in the papers, and it would make Mother happy."

"I can't just at present."

Although the head was completely engulfed in a helmet and a somewhat noisome (is that what I mean? – like my brother's Afro) complex of tea towels, I had correctly identified the voice.

"I do not see anything that is being done here that could not be done as well in your absence for a time. There are voices enough to inform Sister Blanche of your plans. (Pulverize her? Really!) Yours is not needed, except possibly to make it sound more like her funeral."

"A black wave of death. That is what they are. Sister Blanche and all of them. Black waves of death, all of them."

"You have not answered my objection."

"You know what they do to informers."

"Beat them about the head and shoulders, until they are insensate and more, with collapsible lead pipes. That is what they do. But you would not be an informer."

"They would not know it. We do not go away save in threes and fives. She who goes in one must pay the price."

"Well, come in threes and fives. The more, Mother has always said, do you not remember, the merrier."

"It would be a contradiction."

That gave me pause. I used it to inform myself, from all the posters and billboards and throwsaway that stood and lay about, what it was that had them in such a state. It did certainly seem that Sister Blanche was asking for pulverization. White Lily was behaving in a quite anile manner. All of the intellectual circles, the Circle for the Cuban Thing and the Black Friday Circle and the rest, must call it a day no later than two in the morning, and by that hour all persons not possessing Lily White credentials, by which is meant men, must have departed the Yard (as it is called). (So silly! Who would do mischief to a White Lily? As well to a tree stump, Mr. Madder used to say, evocatively.)

"Come at two in the morning, when the circles disband. Pretend you are a Black Friday."

"My hair is not right."

"It would make Mother happy."

"The world is full of unhappy mothers, many of them for less cause."

"That is true." Before sincerity, all fades into irrelevance, which is what Zen is about.

"Do me a favor. I had thought of writing, but it is difficult. A letter must make its way past things. Bring me the foot locker in my closet."

I could not remember that she had ever brought *me* a foot locker. I nonetheless made responsive query: "Where?"

"The southwest cubicle of the public convenience nearest the Japanese garden at Hibiya Park. You will find me, waiting. Knock on the door."

"When?"

"At three in the afternoon."

"If you can go to the southwest cubicle, etc., at three in the afternoon, why then can you not come home?"

"We will be in threes and fives."

"Will there be room for all of you?"

"There always has been."

"When, then, as I have asked already, can you not come home, in those same threes and fives?"

"And have them *see*?"

This was true. Besides, the hour for the reunion was at hand. My classmates would be exchanging fond memories of all that had obtained since the last reunion, and I did not want to miss them, or the opportunity to offer a few of my own. (And what a fortnight for international cultural exchange it has been, too!)

I vouchsafed a single query further; "What is in the locker?"

"Parts."

I think that my sister's discontent might strike you as more quantifiable than my own, and that is why I write to you of her. I do hope that the two of you will meet one day, when all this torment is over.

The poem has shaped itself. This event occurred back just there where the southwest cubicle entered my transcript.

> Of *Daphne odora* the scent is nostalgia,
>> *Mal du pays*
>> For other days,
> Yes, even the dullest American nose tells you.

(Or am I wrong?)

Do not forget that the season is a captious, whimsical one. "Spring," the calendar and the almanac may announce, but there is yet winter in the air. Do, I pray you, resist all impulses to fling things off.

13. Miss Gray to Mr. Brown

I arose this Sabbath morning with a sense of urgency. Our birthday and that of the nation is only two days off, and I have not yet wished you, and it, a happy one. I do hope that it will be a happy one, for both of you.

I write also to tell you that the weather has been glorious. The moss in the dingles is its loveliest. You do not have the likes of it in Tokyo, for you do not have the Central Node to protect you from Russian winds.

Our moss here got sat upon, by Miss Kurozora, who, with retinue, came calling yesterday morning.

> Oh they come in ones but they came in tens,
> The Choopy Wrens, the Choopy Wrens.

There were photographers and reporters to the right and local Choopies to the left of our moss-bordered garden path, and in came Miss Kurozora, late in the morning, followed by a stately Tokyo retinue.

She did not look at the photographers and reporters and she did not look at the local Choopies; and then, abruptly, she halted, and turned to the retinue. There was a conference. At the end of it, one of the Tokyo Choopies raised an umbrella, took aim, and struck one of the photographers.

My landlady was beside me, missing little. Her Japanese being better than mine, I asked what had happened. She began her explanation by quoting a famous piece of light verse from the Edo Period, which I may translate for you as follows:

> Out enjoying the
> Evening cool. How good to be
> A he, not a she.

The photographer had quoted the second sentence, but in his version the she state was advanced as the better of the two. The meaning of the standard version, which I think charming, is that at the end of a hot afternoon a man can throw off his work-day clothes and go out loosely and scantily clad, but this is not permitted a woman. The photographer's version, which I like too, carried very strongly the implication that the world would pay little heed to Miss Kurozora were she not a she.

My landlady was unable to eavesdrop upon the conference that preceded resort to the umbrella, but doubtless it had to do with whether reverence for the high priesthood of the mass media should prevail, or outrage at the insult to The Movement.

I do not know who knocked Miss Kurozora to our mossy earth. My landlady thinks that it was those awful Tokyo people, that the cordon which they formed between Miss Kurozora and the photographers was altogether too muscular.

There upon the moss, in any event, she was.

"I have been guilty," came an imperious voice, "of a great breach of decorum."

She was now upon her knees, and she had twisted about on the moss, doing it great damage, so that she was facing the house and me.

"I have been guilty of a great breach of decorum," she said again, more imperiously, getting to her feet.

She then seemed to rise slightly into the air, and by a process akin to levitation, I should think, took herself back to the footpath without further disturbing the moss.

Simultaneously my landlady leapt from the veranda and into the footgear beneath, scarcely displacing them. I have marveled at the skill with which Kabuki actors slip into footgear. This was every bit as good.

"There can be no excusing the discourtesy to which an ancient visitor, I mean a distinguished visitor to our ancient capital, has been subjected," said my landlady, brushing vigorously at a mossy haunch. "By way not of apology but of explanation it may be pointed out that not everyone in our ancient capital is of the stock of that ancient capital."

Had I been a Kyoto Choopy Wren, for it was at the Kyoto Choopy Wrens that her glare was directed, I would I think have flown on shattered wing and sought a place to expire.

"Oh pray do not say so," said Miss Kurozora, with a yet greater access of imperiousness. "We must all of us learn to know our places in the world, and I have today been taught a valuable lesson in the matter. I must thank you for it, and apologize for the impertinence which brought me to your beautiful city. I think that I will not make so heedless a mistake again. I look forward to receiving you, Gray, at National Headquarters of The Choopy Wren in Tokyo." The capital letters are in my original.

"May I offer you a cup of tea?" said I, foolishly.

"To have a cup of American tea with you was until a moment ago the event upon which my expectations focused. But other events have intervened. They may have been puzzling to you, a guest of our narrow and in many ways benighted land. If that be the case, I am very sorry indeed, and shall seek ways to make amends when next I see you at National Headquarters of The

Choopy Wren in Tokyo. Doubtless you have your down-to-earth American reasons for having chosen to live in this place of remembered glory. I look forward to hearing of them on the day when next it is my privilege to receive you at National Headquarters of The Choopy Wren in Tokyo."

"Not for everyone," said my landlady, "is the glory of our ancient capital a remembered thing; but the ineffability which makes it, for some of us, present and palpable is not, I fear, to be conveyed to the person from the hinterlands who is visiting for the first time. I have often said, indeed, and for this very reason, that no one should visit our ancient capital for the first time. The pity that you were not warned rises within me and threatens to engulf me, and I can but say once more that no chain of apologies, however complex, could be adequate."

"No more, I pray you, no more. The fault is mine for failing to remain where we of an idealistic bent belong. It is I who must apologize, knowing that no apologies can be adequate for such a failure of prescience."

"Would that I might send a magician off in search of an elixir, that this deplorable incident be erased from your memory, and with it all the misconceptions about our ancient capital which prevail in the hinterlands."

"In this erstwhile but now neglected city, where memory must be replied upon to maintain a precarious sense of direction, you propose too great a sacrifice. The memory will be added to all the others which give your city its very special quality. No more, I do indeed pray you, no more."

That was that. She departed, and International Cultural Exchange had had a bad day.

> How it grieves us, you and me,
> All us who love it, I.C.E.,
> That it should have the shattered day
> It had on yester Saturday.
> Oh may it have a gladder day
> On Monday, than on Saturday.

If she had consulted an almanac she would have come in the

afternoon and not in the morning, and everything would have been all right; but of course she is not an almanac type.

I will raise a cup, you may be sure, to us and our birthday, and to the nation and its. How nice if we could celebrate together. On the other hand, there cannot be too many occasions for letters, containing poems.

I enclose a copy of Miss Shiraito's of the Nineteenth Night. It will not tell you a great deal about House of Craft and the happenings which most interest you, but should a peanut or two fall into place, good. As for the demurrer, I offer no opinion.

If it is true that weather moves from west to east, then you may be assured of at least one more glorious day. Enjoy it, and do have a good birthday.

14. Mr. Brown to Miss Gray

I have waited until the very eve of our birthday to offer felicitations. I am learning about these things, and wanted to have a genuinely felicitous day. Today is such a one, and the eve, as well, of the lunar New Year, which we in California, victims of some lobby or other, call the Chinese New Year. Your letter was delivered late this morning. I must say that a thing they manage well is the delivery of express mail. I thank you very much.

Tomorrow promises to be an early-vernal sort of day. The willows down by the lake are all glaucous, not much different in color, I should think, from your moss, before Choopy depredations.

> Oh some are singles and others are groupies,
> Choopies erect and fallen Choopies,
> Upright Choopies and the downright Choopies.

I look back over this year of my life, another year of trying to be a newspaperperson, and find myself almost wishing for a transfer, and envious of Miss Shiraito. The editors of the *Morning Flush*, as they scan her contributions, care only that she agrees with them. Then they print her, and they give her ingenious umbrellas. Meeting her on a rainy day, you will find her with an object that seems designed for shelter, of course, and for all manner of secret gratification as well.

My editors are less understanding. I cannot persuade them that businessmen so much more competent than our own are going to create problems, and therefore are news. Dying giants in Peking are news, and so are munificent tyrants in Seoul; but this nation of businessmen, so awful in its successes, is not.

Yet I think I may be coming upon something good. Thank you for the copy of Miss Shiraito's letter of the Nineteenth Night. The evidence gathers that the fifteenth floor of House of Craft is a place where things happen. I went there once, but could not find a place to sit, and now go rather to the library, on the twelfth floor. Sometimes she sits beside me, and we read the *Wall Street Journal.*

"Is it one of those foreign words we have made over into our own, like 'avec' and 'sequin'?" asked she, beside me, some days ago.

"What word?" asked I, knowing full well.

"'Peanuts.' Here it is in the *Wall Street Journal.* The former governor is making a great deal of money with his peanuts. (Isn't that nice. I must tell my mother.) But it never seems to mean what Mr. Kuromaku and Mr. Minawata have it mean."

"What do they make of a peanut?"

"A million, I think, figuring backwards. I am good at figuring backwards. It is the way my father taught me to do my income tax."

"So?"

"You speak better the Japanese than we Japanese do."

I could not think of another thing to say. I never can, when the remark is made. Can you?

With me it has this little way,
The popular

> Vernacular,
> Spectacular-
> Ly stopular
> Of any other thing to say.

To her credit, she does not say it as often as most of them do. Perhaps the possibility came to her that we were being bugged, and she wanted to be on record with the correct thing.

Tell me about your birthday, and I will tell you about mine. I have learned that I was born in the Year of the Chicken. I have learned further that in this fact is everything the world needs to know about me. I hope I am not right in thinking that you are one or two years younger than I, for if I am then you were born in the Year of the Dog or the Year of the Pig. Now for the Dog and for the Pig, the best time has passed. It was the time of the great student struggle, when the Dog received a great deal of attention on this side of the water, and his cousin the Pig on the other. What Pig, what Dog, can be greatly excited about the struggle now unfolding in White Lily Yard?

15. Miss Shiraito to Mr. Brown

Happy, happy birthday!

I think I shall write this dark, moonless winter night away! I think I shall write the night away, and likewise the morning too!

Seldom can there have been such a conjunction of felicitous elements. Your birthday falls on the First Day of the First Month, which is to say, New Year's Day, by the lunar reckoning. And spring has come both the lunar way and the solar, thus eliminating the cause of perplexity at the heart of the poem I translated for you in my last letter. I hope that you did not fret over it immoderately.

As for the fiction that it, your birthday and Professor Gray's, is also the anniversary of the foundation of our nation, it were

41

better forgotten. You might think, from the fuss that is made, that the day is ours alone. It is not.

> Nothing could be finer
> Than to have it go to China,
> Asia Major, Asia Minor,
> And at length to Carolina,
>> In the morning.
> Move the dateline to the west,
> And we might have it last,
>> And they the sooner of this Lunar New Year's
>>> morning.

I think it important to remember these things, and to call them to the attention of the jingoists. I enclose a copy of a letter to the *Morning Flush* giving the correct view of the matter. The *Flush* is certain to carry numbers of letters giving the correct view, and I hope that mine will be among them.

There is yet another felicitous coincidence (what a day!): the First Day of the First Month, or, by the lunar reckoning, New Year's Day, is also the First Day of the Rat, for courtiers of old a day of gay rejoicing. They scampered about pulling up pine trees and then planting them again. How I wish we could have been with them, you and I! What fun we would have had! Searching for an appropriate poem, I come upon a famous poet making inquiry of certain pine trees:

> And on what ancient Day of the Tiger
> Were you implanted, O pines of Shiga?
> Nay, 'twas not then, nor the Day of the Cow,
> That we were put where we are now,
> Nor that of the Rabbit, or Chimpanzee,
> That we were put where we seem to be.
> And was it then the Day of the Cat?
> There is no such. 'Twas the Day of the Rat
> That we were put where we are at.

I have expanded and embroidered, somewhat. It is my theory that something is lost in translating a Japanese poem, and that

42

something should be added by way of compensation, especially for foreigners.

I was happy to find you at home last night, and so agile, despite the badger incident; and doubly happy that I found you about to depart your writing desk; and doubly happy, as well, at your reception of my birthday present, which balances the grapefruit nicely, I think. Though inclined to doubt that you did well to prune the grapefruit, I said to myself, "He is from California."

It was thoughtful of you to keep pointing out that I had a hard day ahead. As a matter of fact I had less sleep than you might have expected me to have, after we made our farewells. There was an incident. It was one of the things that happen, and would not be worth remarking upon were it not for our differences about Governor Minobe. Tokyo is not as easy a city to govern as you think it is. Less genius is required than you think to govern it badly.

I had no trouble finding a cab down by the lake. The driver was one of the chatty ones. He offered opinions on a number of subjects.

On Foreign Minister Gromyko: "A thief at a fire" (cf. Kenkyusha's Japanese-English Dictionary, third edition, page 665).

On garbage: "Take it back to the western suburbs where it belongs. You people make the mess. Why should we be the ones to live with the smell?"

A glance at his license revealed him to be from your eastern portion of the city.

On Governor Minobe: "The only way to get rid of him is to get rid of woman suffrage. He's still a little way off from the grave." (Again the translation is Kenkyusha's. I will comment upon it in a moment.)

I have nothing to learn from such people. I know it, and long have known it. The remark about Governor Minobe sent me into a reverie about – us! My tapes establish that I listened well to you, and remembered well your pithy American remarks. It was from these last that my reverie had its point of departure.

I was presently shaken from it. Not listening, I had been making harmless reply to the driver. (I think that you Americans are only just beginning to awaken to the importance of tapes. It is a matter in which we have been ahead of you.)

He elaborated upon the theme of the grave at what might have seemed morbid length had the language not been Japanese. His word for "grave" was a designation of apertures so general that the Kenkyusha entry (see page 25 of the third edition) occupies upwards of half a column.

It was done with ingenuity and imagination, I must say, and a profusion of associative imagery.

"Well, one cannot be sure," I would say; and: "It may be true for aught I know"; and "Certainly such things are open to question and criticism."

"It is dissatisfaction with their husbands that makes women vote for Minobe. Are you dissatisfied with your husband?"

"Now that you mention it."

"Which are you dissatisfied with? What he does or what he does not do?"

"Start to finish."

"Both."

"After a manner of speaking."

"Lady yesterday told me an interesting thing. She said that in her apartment house the salesmen and delivery boys –"

"There are such, too, I believe, among others."

"How often?"

"In season, and out of season, as well."

"How about a poor, hard-working taxi driver for a change?"

"Variety is the spice of life, they say. I believe I have heard them say it."

Imagine my surprise, if you will, at a female voice shrilling: "Welcome! Welcome!" It was what roused me from my reverie.

We were before an establishment whose glass doors bore the emblem, the upside-down jellyfish, as it is called, which upon maps signifies spas. Now there are no spas within scores of miles of Tokyo. (Let us go to one, some time, you and I, off in the mountains.) In Tokyo the emblem signifies an inn of questionable character. (Be on your guard against it.)

The driver had opened his automatic door, that from which the passenger descends, and was making elaborate gestures as of fanning a fevered brow. The maid seemed to understand, too well, perhaps, indeed, it may have been. It may have been that they were not strangers.

"There, now," she said. "It will wear off. Just come in, do, and have a nice drink of Kalpis. And where," she said, aiming her query midway between me and the driver, who, having descended, had me by the other arm, "have you been disporting?"

The more I think of it the surer I am that they were acquainted. Upon his cap was the emblem of his company, a bat out of hell. Such drivers must drive indefatigably to support themselves. Supporting permits of no disporting. He had to be at the end of his time of duty. Otherwise things made no sense. Such a pert one as she was!

You are fair-minded enough, I think, to see what the incident, the rest of it routine, demonstrates: that Tokyo is not easy to govern. The things that can happen to a girl, through no fault of her own, in the Tokyo night!

> You might not be so disapprobic
> Of urban arrangements Minobic,
> Had it been your plight
> To be out in the night
> In predicaments scyphozophobic.

I almost believe that it is beginning to snow, this morn of your birthday. I will think of the snow as another good omen. May the snows accumulate, as the years of your pilgrimage!

> And should the scent of *Prunus* now
> Permeate the covering snow,
> Who will break us off a spray?
> I do not know, I cannot say.
> Who will break us off a bough?
> I cannot say, I do not know.

45

Such pleasure as there is in these ancient questions, and in the delicious uncertainty of the replies!

Happy birthday! Happy, happy birthday! Happy Lunar New Year's Day!

15a: The enclosure to Miss Shiraito's letter

Is it a Day for Rejoicing?

Shiraito Yoko

(Salaried person, Tokyo, age 22)

Is it a day for rejoicing? No. This must be the answer, the answer of all the millions of mothers who lost sons (for the most part) in the recent war.

One's heart cannot fail to burn with anger at the scenario before us. It is as follows: the politicians who were responsible for the lamentations of all these mothers now tell us that it is a day for rejoicing. Can such cynicism be permitted? No. One's heart burns with anger.

"Three can make a tiger." This is a piece of ancient wisdom from our great neighbor to the west. Do you know what it means? It means that when three people assert the existence of a tiger the whole village commences accepting it as fact. How many people roam freely about with reports of fictitious tigers in our own village? It is they who tell us that this is a day for rejoicing. They succeed with the fraud because for them the people are a convenience, etc., and no more. My heart burns with anger.

We will have an election shortly. In this election, the anger of us upon whom is being perpetrated the fraud can be converted into force if the factions of the opposition, of greater and lesser degree, will only join together. Why do they not?

In the land to the west of us, a frog is reported to have remarked (and I quote): "The sky is no bigger than the mouth of a well." To this erroneous statement, Chairman Mao Tse-tung offered a sententious corrective: "If it had said, 'A part of the sky is the size of the mouth of the well,' that would be true, for it tallies with the facts."

Let us take to heart this corrective.

It is no day for rejoicing.

Yet there is a sense in which it is. It is the birthday of Mr. Daniel Boone, Mr. Thomas Alva Edison, Mr. George Brown of the *Los Angeles Times*, and Professor Hilda Gray of Redrock State University. Let us rejoice for and with them.

16. Miss Shiraito to Miss Gray

On this joyous morning, cloaked all in white, as if to emphasize that our joy contains no suspect coloring and yet contains all the hues and tones of good wishes: on this snowy morning I offer you a poem written by, and, I may say, fit for, a queen, on this lunar New Year's morning.

> Cometh spring time, notwithstanding the presence
> of snow,
> And, *Horeites diphone*, thy tears now may thaw.

And it is your birthday, and Mr. Brown's!

> Grow old, a thousand years, eight thousand, older,
> While little pebblet grows to mossy boulder!

This verselet, exactly commensurate with my wishes for you and Mr. Brown, is everywhere heard on this day, for it is held by some to be our national anthem, even as, by some, the day is held to be the anniversary of the founding of the land. No one can say with a certainty that it *is* in fact our national anthem. It is one of those things. So here we are.

Snow is yet falling. It is a very windless snow, and the branches and the twigs trace sinuous ridges of white. Now and again a branch of *Pinus pentaphylla var. komatsu* rears itself like a surging, rampant thing in all the whiteness.

I interrupted myself to go for the *Morning Flush*, but

someone had been there before me. Now this is strange, thought I, for my father prefers to read Chinese early in the morning, and to have his bad news, as he calls it, at breakfast. My mother declines to look at it until after he is finished, and in any event shows a continuing interest only in the stock market. Neither my younger older brother nor my younger sister is in residence at the moment. So I thought it strange.

But not for long. My father had preceded me into the breakfast room.

"You know I had a feeling that that other Miss Shiraito would be favoring us on this most feudal of mornings. I was right. I was right too in supposing that her heart would, this lovely cold snowy morning, burn with anger. I really do wish that you could get in touch with her, and suggest that she change her name, offering, of course, as would only be fair, to pay court costs. I doubt that many people who know you could think you capable of such nonsense. A few might."

"I agree with her." I felt it incumbent to stand by my opinion, of which please find a copy enclosed.

"Do you, now. I rather like the part about the tiger and the part about the frog. But I do not like to have these things said about our politicians, who are good politicians, giving us exactly what we deserve. In the matter of the grieving mothers I defer to your grandmother. How strange that all those Americans should have the same birthday, and *such* a birthday. I wonder what their fathers had in mind, way over there. Ask, when next you meet."

"Ask whom?" said I, prettily.

"Why whom but Mr. George Brown and Miss Hilda Gray? I would like to meet the former myself, some time. If that other Miss Shiraito were you, why I am sure he would be just the sort of pink plump foreigner she would be throwing herself at. Not that I would not like to meet Miss Hilda Gray as well."

So you see you will receive a warm welcome, at any time that you find it convenient to come.

Mr. Brown seems cheerful, despite the badger incident.

We are informed that Kong Kong measles are abroad. The

assaults upon our sex are said to be more considerable than upon the other, causing mutations. I hope that neither have you been a victim, nor relaxed your guard.

17. Mr. Brown to Miss Shiraito

Such lovely weather as we are having, and each willow thread down by the lake is putting out buds, and all the little sparrows are having dust baths, and I wonder why. I notice these things, now that we have become friends. As I jog around the lake I say to myself: "One of these days I will be writing to Miss S. And how shall I begin?" I thank you for this.

That I am jogging once more is my happy news. The badger did not, you see, cause permanent damage. Thank you for bringing that supply of Chinese cures. The variety was very great, you were too kind. I concluded that one of the principles of Chinese medicine must be to fight bile with bile. Few countries can have been more diligent in finding uses for uncomely creatures. My Aunt Lucy used to say: "Leave my bats and spiders and snakes alone. They are there for a reason." Do you think she might have been a Chinese physician in a former life?

And the *Citrus tachibana*, and the grapefruit, and the *Citrus trifoliata*, and the badger. And now has commenced a stream of wellwishers inspired by your letter, on my recent birthday and Hilda's, to the *Morning Flush*. There is no end to your kindness.

That I am jogging is my happy news. Were you to see me doing so one of these mornings, however, you might ask a series of related questions:

> Oh what is the matter with Mr. Brown?
> He wears a semi-quavering frown.
> What *is* the matter with Mr. Brown?

49

He looks not up, he looks but down,
Unmoved by all the citily sounds
In which this most citily city abounds.
Why wears he this febrile, fretful frown,
Our erstwhile cheerful Mr. Brown?
Does "friendly embarrassment" get him down
(Sometimes almost to the ground)?

We some of us play a game. It is one that you should like, sesquipedalian Miss Shiraito. One person gives a definition from Kenkyusha (so full of them) and the others try to guess the Japanese original. Within the quotation marks in my last lyrical line but one (see above) I have set you a problem. Let me know when you have the answer. We can meet for lunch, or one of those Foojy House surprises.

Saps ascend, sometimes, it may seem, all too vigorously. It is a thing about Tokyo saps. One must be on one's guard.

18. Miss Gray to Mr. Brown

The weather maps inform me that you are having bright, sunny weather. Chairman Mao was wrong. It is not the east wind but the west that prevails. If you are not a devotee of weather maps yourself, I must warn you of chilly, rainy weather in the space of a few days. It is what we are having. The city is very sombre in these rains of early spring. I hope you will not accuse me once more of sounding like a tea ceremony when I say that in the sombreness there is great beauty. There is.

I have had callers in large numbers, because of Miss Shiraito's letter to the *Morning Flush*. I am sure that you have had far more. In these matters we hayseeds cannot hope to compete with you of the great metropolitan center. They come bearing gifts and they come bearing conversation manuals and they come bearing the *Morning Flush*, which they ask me to autograph, quite as if I had written it. They come telling me that I must be lonely so far from home, even though the heaps of shoes in the hallway should inform them that solitude does not prevail. Sometimes, listening between the lines from the conversation manuals, I detect this sort of message: "Why, O Yankee, do you not go home?" But it is not often. Kindness and concern predominate. Most of my callers are young ladies. Why is this? Is there something about me, or about them?

Miss Shiraito has informed me of a certain badger incident, but given me none of the details. I have mental pictures of you lying mangled and stitched, having ventured heedlessly into a lair. What was it, this incident?

I will be going to Tokyo again next month. I would as soon not stay at Cosmopolitan Culture House this time. It is so overrun with bridesmaids, and then I keep seeing people I would as soon not see, such as Professor What's-his-name.

> I've had enough of Culture
>   Internationale,
> Its hordes of bores and bridesmaids,
>   Bánal and banál.

Do you have suggestions? I cannot afford to put up at any of the grand hotels. It used to be that I had a little more money than a few Japanese, but no more.

The weather maps bring a certain disquiet. I have a picture of you not only mangled and stitched, but sunburned as well. Do apply ointments.

19. Mr. Brown to Miss Gray

Yes, the weather has been fine. Today we enter the Time of Rainwater, this almanac informs me. Its division of the calendar into delicately shaped bits and particles pleases me very much; but the Time of Rainwater, coming at one of the sunniest seasons, when the blossoms of *Prunus* swell and burst, makes me think that a Chinese influence is at work. The "Americanization" which French ambassadors so lament must answer to an ancient need, once satisfied by Chinese things, and now by American.

The badger incident is as follows.

On an evening when I was out Miss Shiraito left a great hulk of a ceramic badger with the watchman. It gave me quite a start, but I struggled into the elevator with it. As we ascended I was taken with a wish to see where anything so – emphatic – might have been fabricated. I tipped it back to look at the potter's mark, which I found on the under side of the penetralia, and which informed me that it is from your part of the country. Setting it aright once more, I gave my back a wrench so painful that I had to summon the neighborhood physician, a good, patient man who does not seem to mind being out at all hours. People say that he has voted for Governor Minobe in the past and will do so again in the election before us, but I do not mind, as long as he goes on being good and patient. He took me off to his clinic, where I was given an injection and someone walked up and down my spine for a while. I was in greater pain when I came out than when I went in, but I soon began to recover, and now have recovered almost fully.

The badger is hideous. Few things wrought by god or man have been more so. It wears on its head one of those berets which intellectuals affect upon returning from France, and on its face a ghastly simper. And the penetralia are Monstrous.

> Avast, avast with badgers
> > Philoprogenital!
> And what was that, and what was *that*?
> > My dear, it was a ball!

I was not angry with her because of the badger incident. Because of her more recent doings I have been somewhat annoyed.

I have had a flood of callers, brought on by her letter to the *Morning Flush*. They have driven me out of home, out of office, and to drink. When one has neither home nor office, the drinking places exercise a powerful attraction. (Such friendly, noisy places.)

Why you should attract young ladies and I should attract them as well, I cannot really say. It is mostly young ladies one sees watching the female impersonators at the Kabuki Theater and it is mostly young ladies one sees watching the male impersonators at the Takarazuka, and so I suppose we may conclude that young ladies are more strongly drawn to oddities than are young men.

Yet it is an ill wind, Miss Gray, from which the cooper does not profit. I have learned a great deal. Drinking places are among the finest for collecting information, in which Craft and its hanky and panky often figure. A Japanese newspaper reporter in his cups is such a mine of information that you come to acquire a new attitude towards the news. You come to see it as something with which to regale audiences in drinking places, but something to keep out of newspapers, because once it is in them the audiences cease to be regaled. Try reading the *Flush* with this principle in mind. You will understand it better.

And just look at all these presents, if you will.

> *Ursus hokkaidensis*
> And *Dolli kyushuensis*
>> And senna (stinkweed) tea and gluten cake.
> A birch stump from Nagano
>> And ginseng koreano
>> And fish-gut paste like Mother used to make.
> Matsushima Bay
> And Foojy *repoussé*
>> And haiku on a length of burlap awning.
> But back to *hokkaidensis:*
> I've yet to take a census.
>> Don't underestimate the *Flush of Morning*.

The dolls simper ghastlily up at the badger, and he simpers ghastlily down at them. I thought at first that I liked the native ones better than the foreign ones, but I think so no longer. The former have the worse simpers.

You will ask where, if it is as bad as all that, I found a place to write at such length. Well, I am at home, and I have been writing for quite a spell, as you can see, and of course it is *not* as bad as all that. The doorbell has not rung in some time. There has been a very nice gibbous moon all evening. Whether there is a relation between the silence and the moon, I do not know.

20. Miss Shiraito to Miss Gray

The twigs of the forsythia experience spring swellings, and is it one's imagination that the twigs of the cherries do so as well? The urge is strong, these lovely spring days, to disencumber oneself (as the poet said) and gambol. The season is, however, perhaps the one among them all which most cleverly feigns and misleads. Do not for a moment let this fact stray from your attention.

And it is the second full moon of the year. One of the greatest of our lyric poets indicated a wish to die under a full moon of spring; but there are better things to do, I think, perhaps.

> Under the full moon
> Of the second month,
> I wish not to die
> But to –

Does anything at all rhyme with "month"?

Mr. Brown has sufficiently recovered from the badger incident that we were able to take sweets together yesterday in Fuji House. He took an Everyman's Juice and I a Cornmush Surprise Royale. He told me numbers of things to make me happy, such as that my recent letter to the *Flush* brightened his birthday. But the most gladdening thing in the medley was that you will be coming to Tokyo! You will be coming to Tokyo, and you are looking for a place to stay, having wearied of Cosmopolitan Culture House, where there are too many bridegrooms and professors. I agree with you about the bridegrooms, but one does sometimes come upon the cutest blue-eyed professor. In any event you must stay with us. You must! I have spoken to my mother, and she says very well, and I have already given you my father's views. You can have the room of my younger sister, of whom more in a moment. I take full responsibility and will go through it with counters and detectors.

I followed the instructions, in the matter of my sister, which I reported to you in my last letter but one. I took the foot locker to the specified nook in Hibiya Park. Mr. Brown keeps asking how I managed to transport the badger to his apartment house. Well, I did the same with the foot locker. I shook it well from side to side, and the contents sounded like pickles and preserves.

I went and knocked upon the appointed door. A pleasant young man emerged. Doubtless he had his reasons for being on the ladies' side of the partition and not the gentlemen's. In any event, we Japanese do not make much of such distinctions.

He said he hoped I was enjoying my day of rest.

"Our rest together is in the dust," I replied. "Job 17, 16."

Now this sort of exchange is always pleasant, but I was not helped towards the achievement of my goal.

I sat disconsolately on the foot locker. Numbers of people, passing in and passing out, asked if I might be ill. There were more gentlemen than ladies. I suppose nothing interesting obtained on their side of the partition. I smiled sweetly and thanked them for their solicitude, and said that I was waiting for Godot. (What else could I say?) A policeman passed in. He had a Sendai accent, and immediately I was in stitches. That is the effect Sendai accents have on us Tokyo people. My grandmother has one. She is wonderful at funerals. She soon has the widow in stitches.

"What does that sturdy-looking trunk contain," asked he.

". . ." replied I, restraining my mirth.

"Let me have the key."

". . . ."

"That sturdy-looking trunk does not seem at all a comfort-

55

able place upon which to be reclining. Perhaps I may suggest that you remove yourself, in the interest of your comfort, and my wish, in pursuit of my duties, to learn its contents, here in a crowded nook of a public park."

". . . ." Knowing my rights, I this time added to my reply a curled lip. I took out a cigarette and leaned languorously back upon the foot locker.

For a moment I feared that, like so many other young persons, I might be a victim of police brutality.

But "Fie" said he, briefly, and moved on. (Cf., *che*, Kenkyusha's New Japanese-English Dictionary, third edition, p. 122: "tut!; shocks!; phew!; pshaw! fie!; phooey!; tcha!" Which do you like best? I hesitated between "tcha!" and "fie!") Upon his face, as he turned away, he wore a Sendai expression.

The place was indeed becoming crowded. The time seemed to have arrived when people congregate. So I took up the foot locker and resumed my languorous pose beside a bed of decorative cabbage, beneath a charred ginkgo tree, charred, I think, from fire, quite possibly those cruel fire bombs of yours.

I was looking up meditatively and wondering whether Mr. Brown likes ginkgos when there came a crescendo of chanting from the direction of the latrine patronized by the subway crowd. It was that antiphonal *Sprechchor* used by student groups. In hypnotic antiphony, they were chanting: "Pulverize/the Revolutionary Marxist Union of the Peasant, Worker, and Intellectual!" and: "Pulverize/the Cadre of the Young People's Democratic Republican Progressive Movement!" and: "Pulverize/the Latin-American Afro-Asian Mutual Self-Defense Popular Cooperative Bund!" I wish all you Americans could have heard them. No longer would you have thought of likening the political maturity of Japan to that of a thirteen-year-old.

And how I do wish you could have seen the snake-dancing that emerged from the shrubbery' I am told that sincere students in other parts of the world have taken up the Japanese snake-dance. How nice.

Meanwhile from a southeasterly direction, over beyond the

beds of ornamental cabbage, had come another *Spechchor:* "Pulverize/ the Revolutionary Marxist Anti-Feudal All-Persons-Are-Siblings Federation." They converged upon each other, and upon me, quite as if I had been placed there, and my foot locker, for the purpose. There was a moment of swirling violence and I found myself hoisted with my own petard, or more properly, my sister's. When stillness was restored, in the kinetic sense, I was hanging from a utility pole, my belt having become hooked over one of those proclivities by which utility persons ascend.

Quite a thing was spread out beneath me. There were fingers in eyes and ears and throats, twisted necks and arms, knees in solar plexi and elsewhere, flailing staves and limbs and collapsible lead pipes, sailing helmets and halberds. Certain of you American experts have told us that these are but the games that young people play. Well, blood was flowing as a result of this particular game, I may tell you, a crimson tide, as they say down in 'Bama.

The riot police had come, but they seemed far more concerned to protect the beds of ornamental cabbage than to contemplate bund and cadre and what they were doing to each other. I grew very angry, watching.

And then it was all over, save for the work of the ambulance technicians.

> We may work from sun to sun,
> But an ambulance technician's work is never done.

I was taken down by a policeman with another Sendai accent.

"Be a good girl," he said, giving me a pat upon a jean.

I smiled, half in amusement and half in sadness, the latter half the Japanese smile which, in its complete form, you foreigners find so puzzling. It was *such* a funny accent! And on the other hand the foot locker was gone!

I only hope that it was spirited off by my sister's faction. I think it is the Latin-American Afro-Asian Mutual Self-Defense Popular Cooperative Bund, but I can seldom remember, all the way to the end. My father says he doubts whether she can either, and it might as well be a bund of monkeys, for all the difference it makes. In this I think he exaggerates.

I sat down disconsolately, and wondered what to do next.

> Beneath a blackened *Ginkgo biloba*
> I sat me down and wept,
> Remembering the cask in which the pickles
> And preserves were kept.

But I could think of nothing to do, and so I took a turn through the park to see if there might be other interesting clashes, and came back home again.

That my sister was a part of the game (so to speak) seems certain. I did not detect her distinctive wail, possibly because I was so far above it all. We have had, however, a visit from an assistant chief of the metropolitan police, a Sendai person who was in kindergarten with my father. My father was out. My mother and I received him in the south Japanese parlor, making use of a foot-warmer. We talked about the weather for a time, and the prospects for the cherry blossoms, in which the police are much interested. Then he said that in the litter at Hibiya Park had been an antique bow which he had recognized immediately as a Sendai fabrication, and upon a hunch he had come to inquire – and he undid the elongated parcel which had made him look as if on his way to a lesson. My mother squealed. I kicked at her foot in the foot-warmer, but got him instead. She ran out to the godown. Yes indeed, she said, running back, despite all my frowns. My great great great great grandfather's bow of *Mallotus japonicus* was missing.

And so, as you Americans say, that fat is in the fan.

My mother has given the police pictures, and said that nothing would please her more than to have them pay a visit, one morning or afternoon, at their convenience, in search of fingerprints. She asked only that they seek, if possible, to defer to her fibrulations, likely to come at the end of the lunar cycle. She has said nothing, leastways in my hearing, to my father. Well, she has done what she has done, and the wave of the future cannot in any case be held back.

Do come and stay with us. My mother needs someone to serve breakfast to. My sister has not returned, and my younger older brother, he whose age and mine so resemble each other, is away for increasingly protracted periods. Do come; out of charity. Not many people come this way.

Changeable as the heart of a man are the elements in this time of lingering winter. So open in the morning, one's pores will by noon have clammed up, and it is of the greatest importance to have a capote or a tippet always within reach. Nothing must be allowed to stand in the way of your visit.

21. Miss Gray to Miss Shiraito

You are very kind. Miss Kurozora has told me, though in such a way as to make me fear that files and procedures might be upset, that she can clear a space for me. It is possible that I would make Choopy points were I to stay with her. I fear that it takes a great deal of experience to judge these things properly, in this land of the "abdominal performance" (Kenkyusha). But I would far rather stay with you.

I have not yet joined the crowds at the Green Window for long-distance reservations. The sight of those crowds, when I go to reconnoiter, makes me think that the right to travel may not be among the inalienable ones.

> Not at all unsympathetic
> To the urge peripatetic,
> I, as I approach the station
> And the virulent contagion,
> Think that it, too democratic,
> Asks a mixture of the static.
> Possibly the way of Peking
> Is the one which we are seeking.

I will have my time at a Green Window one of these

mornings, however, and do not doubt that I will obtain a ticket on a Radiant Express. Please tell your parents how grateful I am and what pleasure the anticipation of your hospitality is giving me.

Thank you for writing to the *Flush* about my birthday and Mr. Brown's. I think that in certain differences between our birthdays may be seen regional differences. I did have callers, but by no means as many, it seems, as he, and altogether more spiritual with their generosity, offering me instructorships and advisory positions of various sorts, none of which I will be able to accept. My time in Japan is drawing to a close. It might have been fun to help the Kyoto Poetry Guild with the Englishing of its verselings and longer lays, or to be of assistance to Tea Across the Sea in its plans for a Bicentennial Party in Boston. I thank you very much for having brought these invitations my way.

I start thinking of ways to repay your kindness. The cherries will be blooming before many more weeks, and they are very beautiful, and the season is to be recommended in other respects. Much of old Kyoto goes away. My landlady is old Kyoto. Her family made its money selling curious medicines a very long time ago, and she is as old Kyoto as – as other people whose families made their money selling curious medicines a very long time ago. It is now that she makes her annual trip to Tokyo, which she says is to be preferred for the next month or so. Kyoto, she says, comes to resemble the hinterlands, and Korea.

I agree with you about the weather. I hope that you are being as careful as I am. I look as if ready for a space voyage.

22. Miss Gray to Mr. Brown

Even to this cold place spring is at length coming. *Brassica rapa var. nippoleifera*, that harbinger of spring, is coming forth, and soon there will be rape, rape, rape all across the parklands and up into the hills. Were you to subdue your prejudices and come for a look, you would be doing yourself a favor. Along the south and east shores of Lake Biwa the rape is as nowhere else upon this earth. It is as if the light of early spring had found its own very favorite color.

The weeks and months do scurry by. Soon April will be with us, and the Feast of the Internal Revenue.

> Thirty days hath September,
> April, June, and November,
> And all the rest have thirty-one, except February,
>   which hath twenty-eight, except in years
>   divisible by four, when it hath twenty-nine,
>   although in centesimal years it hath twenty-eight
>   unless they (the centesimal years) be divisible
>   by four hundred, in which case it hath twenty-nine,
>   thou needst must remember.

> It is one of my favorite verselings.

I think that my birthday celebrations are at length coming to an end. Comparing mine with yours, I note that mine have had more of a participatory quality about them. I am asked to join clubs and services. In a recent letter to Miss Shiraito, I suggested that the difference might be regional, but last night as I lay sleeping the possibility came to me that it might have to do with gender. You are a little boy, to be mothered and cuddled, and I am a little girl, to wash the cups and saucers up and brush the crumbs away.

I think, I say, that my birthday may at length be dying down. It has gone about as far as it can go. Word of Miss Shiraito's letter to the *Flush* has reached and been taken up by them who abjure words. I have been invited by Now and Zen to come and sit a spell.

My time runs out. I will go home earlier than I had planned. Having had the education in the thing of the seasons which one gets at the hands of such persons as Miss Shiraito, I see that I have never really noticed the Redrock summer, the most inviting, which is to say the least harsh, of its seasons. I think I would like to go back and get ready to start noticing. Besides, I have learned all I am likely to learn about Choopies, and I must get myself in readiness to publish or – what rhymes with "publish"? "Rubbish" comes fairly near, I think. Do you?

I am looking forward to my trip, and especially to meeting your badger, which you make sound like such a – like such an *objet*.

23. Miss Shiraito to Miss Gray

The flowers of winter and early spring, the camellia and the *Prunus mume* and the rest, yet linger, and the high flood of spring seems about to come crashing down all about us. Beside a garden pond in these western marches there yet blooms a tiny winter camellia. Farther back in the garden the buds of an early magnolia are like a flock of white herons winging across a spring sky.

Had you noticed that the Time of the Stirring of Bugs has come? It makes a person feel all vibrant and on the alert, and yet it arouses apprehensions. So many of them (the bugs) and us will not last the day.

> Brief as the time in this vale of tears
> Of the dew and of the morning glory
> Is the time of us, and the bug that stirs
> In the same or a similar category.

What pleasures you do give me to look forward to, intensifying it by not telling me when you will arrive!

Our Doll Festival this year brought a happening which made me fear for a moment or two that my younger sister's room might not after all be at your disposal.

My mother got out the festival dolls as usual, and seemed to wait, and in the evening my sister telephoned. Listening and not listening over the kitchen extension, I heard as follows.

"It is I."

"I knew that you would call. Your father is not at home."

"But I suppose this situation will change before the night is over? Such pleasures are as foam upon the water."

"Will you be home yourself?"

"Have there been police?"

"We had them one morning. I have never seen a room so crowded with fingerprints. What were they doing on the ceiling?"

"Practicing."

"Where are you?"

"Not so very near, and not so very far away. Neither near nor far. A person cannot go far these days without flying."

"You did not get enough practice, then?" My mother laughed at her little joke, and then said again: "Will you be home?"

"Do you think the police are listening?"

"No. But ask your father. Come home and ask your father."

"Have you brought out the dolls?"

"Come home and see. Come and ask your sister."

"I just wanted to tell you."

"To tell me what?"

"That if a person wants to go far these days a person has to fly."

This time my mother had no joke at hand.

There had been pauses, and now there came the sound, as of a stirring of hives, which indicates that one's time at a pay telephone is running out. I had guessed from the background noises that she was at a pay telephone. I synchronized my hanging up with my mother's, so that the faint tinkling did not give it away. There was a pause, doubtless while my mother waited to see whether my sister would dial again. Then there came a faint tinkling to indicate that she was dialing herself. I synchronized once more.

"We have no apology to make for the fact that the pandas will be unable to accept further calls this evening," came a recorded voice. "We beg your forebearance and patience, and another try in the morning, preferably after the rush hour."

My mother did not seek to dial again, as she might have been expected to had it been a wrong number. Perhaps, at this point in time, she wanted to hear the voice of the panda, a squeaky thing beloved of the whole nation. I suppose I will never be sure.

Of some interest is this: the background voices over my sister's pay telephone had that Kyoto quality about them – you know, as if the mouth had been crammed with dough or plaster of Paris, and no amount of puling would suffice. Do not let me forget to give you a chart of her dentures. It would be a great pity if you were to meet on a Kyoto street and, like Evangeline and Gabriel, pass on again.

I would give a penny to know what my mother made of that remark about flying. She has said nothing to me, though I do not doubt that she has told my father, and that it has reached the big ears of the police, even if they were not eavesdropping, in that way of theirs.

I look forward to specific details of your visit, and must again warn you of the fickle ways of the season. Gossamers and bikinis are called for one day and tweeds and minks the next. Do please come well provided with both.

24. Mr. Brown to Miss Gray

Hello Ms.
Gray.
Pray,
Have we any pomes
Today?

Let me also sing for you a springtime song:

In this time of vernal blossoms,

It is plum
Nonsense not to see you. Out of
Charity, come.

There at the end of my second line – a pivot word! Join me in
raging at all that must be lost in the translation of Japanese lyric
poetry, shot through, as it is, with pivot words. Everything gets
translated into Japanese, and so this letter will too; and I will be
much interested to see what is done to my springtime song.

But anyway: when *will* you, out of charity, come? Should you
wish to call me at home, dial directly, let the telephone ring
thrice, hang up, and dial again. It is a code which I have
devised, against people who want to give me badgers and
things.

You may have to stay with me. I can shove aside pots in the
orangerie to make space for a cot, and we may hope that if you
start up in the night you will not get a thorn in an eye. Balancing
our breakfast things on this and that part of the badger may he
more of a problem, but we must not admit defeat in advance.
The eight hundred myriad gods of the Shinto faith had their
reasons for giving us badgers. We must seek to discover those
reasons.

The Shiraito family is disturbed, and that is why you may
have to stay with me. Miss S. has been furious with her mother
for having permitted the police to take fingerprints. I suspect
myself that no one who numbers among his kindergarten
classmates an assistant chief of police could have dreamed of
trying to keep them away. In any event, the foot locker of the
Hibiya Incident was recovered, and it contained many of the
things with which amateurs make bombs. So, as we say, you
and I, in our pithily American way, the fat is in the fan. A nice
taxicab driver had smashed open the locker, and spared the
police the trouble. All her father asks of his female children,
says Miss S., is that they get married and keep their names out
of the newspapers, especially that giant among them, the
Morning Flush. An amusing little convention, acquiesced in by
the whole family, has it that our Miss S. has obeyed the

injunction. The other Miss S. now presents a more serious problem, and that is why the family is disturbed. I am inclined to think myself, that it is good at times like this to have kindergarten classmates well up in the police hierarchy. We will see.

One day recently, as we sat in Foojy House, Miss S. exploring the mysteries of her Mohammed Ali Glacé and I mine, she said:

"What is a bagman?"

"Why, why do you ask?"

"To improve my English. Why else? The Oxford English Dictionary gives me one who carries a bag, and a commercial traveler, and, in sporting slang, a bagfox (whatever this may be). Webster gives me, in addition, a sorter, checker, etc., of mailbags. None of these fits the context."

"And what is the context?"

"Mr. Gold was with Mr. Kuromaku and Mr. Minawata yesterday, and I steeped three cups of tea apiece. Mr. Gold, you know, the one you keep seeing in the mirror, he laughed a big New York laugh (as you call it) and said, 'No one knows better than I, or better appreciates, a good bagman.'"

"A big fat New York laugh?"

"Now all of a sudden you are interested, and you never are when I talk about Americans. See, here it is on my list of Pithy Brown Things: 'A big fat New York laugh.'"

Perhaps your attention has wandered, as mine had. Let me remind you of the shaggy New York type I see in the Craft lobby.

I assured her that I did now remember. "I need to know more of the conversation before I can hope to tell you exactly what, in the context, a bagman might be."

"I steeped three cups of tea apiece, as I have told you. The first time Mr. Gold was saying to Mr. Kuromaku and Mr. Minawata that they spoke English better than he, and that was nice. The second time they were speaking again of peanuts. (I *do* think that it may be one of those foreign words we have made our own, like, 'wet' and 'madame' and 'mansion.' Mr.

Gold seems to know exactly what it means. Why do not you?) And then the third time Mr. Gold was congratulating himself, or so it seemed, upon approaching the end of a challenging and delicate task, and there came this thing about a bagman."

"I have not asked you much about Mr. Gold, and you have not told me."

"You never seem interested when I talk about Americans. He is with the Dedlock office out in Puckery Gulch."

"Puckery Gulch?"

"Where I change trains, mornings and evenings. That is what my other American intimate called it. He liked word games too."

So it is that a piece falls here, and a piece falls there, to join it. I do not like to think that I am using a friend. For Miss S. *is* a friend. The trouble is that for her the concept of friendship keeps slopping over into all sorts of other things. Yet she is a friend. If, as my ears stretch forth at the mention of Mr. Gold and his peanuts and his bagman, and Dedlock Aircraft and Turbulines, I am not using her, then what am I doing?

You may find the plums still in bloom, depending on when in the month you come, or the cherries in bud. The time between the two is among the nicest of times. Forsythias and willows stir, and there are dandelions, among my favorite flowers; and we too have rape, here, there, and everywhere. Come when the moon is waxing. It is no time to languish in a provincial city.

25. Miss Gray to Mr. Brown

> Oh how happy I will be
> In the blooming orangerie!

There, now. In the matter of pivot words, I yield place to none. But I must postpone the delights of the orangerie to another time. I maneuvered my way past the Craft switchboard this morning, and was informed by Miss Shiraito that the affairs of the other Miss Shiraito are quiescent, and that I continue to be welcome.

Miss S. thinks that you must go to Korea, in search of atrocities. Must you indeed? Surely the atrocities can wait a few days, or, if they cannot, there will be others. I want very much to see you before I go home, and there may not be another chance. Upon my return to Kyoto I will have these farewell parties, in such uninterrupted procession that I may have to take fright with Turbulines from Osaka and scarcely see Tokyo at all, save through a smog dimly.

I keep wondering whether I have missed something. We used to hear from all manner of people, and still do from Chinese and professors of Chinese, that the Japanese are a nation of imitators. In the realm of taste and sensibility it is plum nonsense. But in the realm of the intellect? There is a certain charm about the way in which my Choopies put together their edifices from rafter to foundation, but I have seen none who proceed in the other direction. Gatherers of artificial flowers from alien lands are my Choopies!

But have I missed something? This is what I would ask you.

This moonless night is the Night of the Brazen Monkey. My landlady and some friends are keeping the Vigil of the Brazen Monkey. It is an old Chinese thing which comes once every sixty days, and believers must stay up all night, lest worms do mischief. I do not for a moment imagine that they are believers. It is just that they think it a pretty tradition which should not be allowed to die. I have been invited to participate, and will soon go down and do so, and all night long we will compose and sing Songs of the Brazen Monkey. I will be asked to compose and sing a song, I know, and must give some thought to being spontaneous; and allowance will be made for the fact that Americans have no ear.

> Oh sing a Song of the Brazen Monkey,
> It does not matter, off or on key.

26. Miss Shiraito to Mr. Brown

From the earth the forsythia sends up a mist of radiant yellow, while from the sky the willows send down a mist of the freshest green, and between is a gap of a meter or so, where man is vile. (The things that do go on!) Everything wears the garments of spring. It is, however, a changeable time. Only native flora really know what to do with these fluctuations and titubations. It is so as well with fauna? I pray that it is not.

As for our holiday today, let us render it as Mid-spring Day. Is there another country, I wonder, in which this day of the equinox is a legal holiday, for this reason and no more, that it is the day of the equinox? Probably not.

So you must go to Korea, you really must, just when Professor Gray is coming to town? I am the cooper who profits from the wind, for I will have her more to myself. Yet I hate to think of you so far away. The image comes to mind, and will not leave, of a band stretched taut and about to give. "But it will not happen, silly girl," I hear you saying, in that American way.

Of course you are right.

> A bowline knot, a harness knot,
> A granny knot, a catspaw knot,
> For worlds and worlds to come, God wot.
> If all of them should pull apart,
> I can but say, "Why this is odd!"

I have tried to assure Professor Gray, and please add your own assurances if you are in communication, that the matter of my sister need not worry her at all. The room will be awaiting her, warm as toast, and we now have the unsolicited opinion of the police that the heat will set nothing off. My mother worries about my sister but says come right ahead if necessary. My father does not seem to worry in the least, and looks forward to a good long talk about Peking man.

He does not seem to worry in the least about my sister, I mean, of course. My brother is the one, my younger older brother. Of him I must tell you, before you set off for Korea.

He came down to breakfast at the usual time, but there had been a change. His Afro had given way to – a blue-black stubble which was there and not there at all! It had, as poets of old would have said, that dewflower look.

"Tcha!" said my father, taking up the *Flush*.

I thought at the time that my brother's purpose was only to make my father say "Tcha!", and that he had succeeded. It is the sort of thing he does. Then I started thinking, and the matter came to seem more inverted.

It used to be that little boys had shaven heads the better to deal with scabs, scales, and scurfs. What little girls did with unshaven heads, I do not remember. They scratched, I suppose. Anyway: when I see a man with a shaven head, I always wonder what it is he wishes to go back to.

"I like it," I said, when Mother had gone down into the garden and Father down into the automobile. "And think of the money you will save. But what does it mean?"

"If you like it, why that is meaning enough."

"It is not the first change I have noticed of late." I did not propose to be put off by this badinage. "You have not been getting as much lately."

"About the same, really."

"That is not true. The pinballs have not been doing as well by you. Your chocolate hutches are measurably lighter."

"This snooping might get you in trouble. Remember that a fondness for explosives runs in the family. In the part of the family we have in common."

"I do not snoop. I know without knowing. You do not bring home the chocolate and tobacco as you used to."

(Both of them American things. I wonder what the Cosa Nostra Pinball Parlor would be giving as premiums if Columbus had not discovered America.)

"More than one explanation is possible."

"I do not think so. A feel for them is a feel for them. You have it or you do not have it. It does not go away. I read it in a book."

"There are ups and downs. I have needed a holiday."

"Have you ever had anything else?"

"That was unkind. But let me explain myself. I think of moving."

"Where?" I always wonder, as I have said, what these people want to go back to.

"Well, not out there, certainly." He nodded towards the garden, where my older older brother lives.

"I will be lonely. Especially at breakfast."

"For a time. But he will start having plans for you. A daughter left behind at the breakfast table does not fit into the system."

Now about my older older brother: he lives out in the garden and I do not know much about his life. What I see tells me that it is the life of the dedicated salaried person. It seems to contain time for many things but none for my brother himself. He comes home from work very late in the evening, and when I look, not looking, into the garden cottage, he and his wife are already in bed. On Sundays there is a pull: will he, on the one hand, go shopping with his wife or take the baby to see the pandas, or will be, on the other, play golf with one of the vice-presidents? He used to be a great reader, back before he passed his last examinations and became a salaried person. He has done all the right things in the way of having interviews and passing examinations, and my younger older brother has done none of them. Now perhaps you know what my younger older brother meant when he nodded towards the garden.

"Maybe you could take me with you. Where do you mean to go?"

"I think you know."

"But tell me."

"To Mother's, the one I have and you do not. Hers is a part of town left behind by economic miracles. On the walls of certain whimsically decorated houses there are still signs in English, from a quarter of a century ago, warning American soldiers to keep away lest they catch something. I hope no one writes a letter to the *Flush* calling them a national disgrace. They ought to be registered as National Treasures."

71

"Is it that she has asked you to live with her?"

"I sometimes think so."

"And will it mean getting away from Father? Do you talk to her about him?"

"I sometimes think so. She sometimes seems to be saying that he has many admirable qualities."

And that is where we are. I wanted to tell you before your departure, that you may mull the problem over, and offer suggestions upon your return; and I am sure that you will welcome something to take your mind from those Koreans.

I hope that you have not been disturbed by my silence about the puzzle you sent me in your last letter. Such an amusing one – but puzzles are not perhaps what I am best at. I thought and thought, and then commenced reading a dictionary, Kenkyusha's fourth. There in the right hand column on p. 39, before I had completed the letter "A," I came upon it *Arigatameiwaku*! *Such* an amusing puzzle! Have others been quicker than I (inadequately sesquipedalian I) with their answers?

Tomorrow is Saturday, which I think of as our day. Do you remember that it was on a Saturday that your pale eyes first looked into my black ones? The honeyed oysters which are the Saturday special at Fuji House are delicious. But of course you are going to Korea and you have told me that I am not to see you off.

27. Mr. Brown to Miss Gray

> Atrocities, atrocities!
> Banzai! those and Prosit! these
> Pure and proud atrocities.

I know I shouldn't, but it is the way I always feel. I am sorry that there are Christian martyrs in Korea and that anger and pity do not consume the whole of my being. I always have such a good time here, that is the trouble.

I saw Miss S. just before my departure. A letter had come by courier, and it contained a plaintive note, and so I called her. We met in Foojy House, where we had the Saturday Special, which I must try to describe for you some time, when the memory is less fresh.

We talked of her brother's affairs, a subject by which I am put into a dilemma.

"My father does not understand," said she, looking melancholily into the depths of her Saturday Special.

"It is a thing you people are always saying. Usually I find that I do not understand what 'understand' means."

"If he would treat my brother as he treats me, then everything would be all right. That is what he does not understand."

"I would have thought, from many things that you have said and written, that you would wish the reverse, to be treated as he is treated."

"That is the idea."

"It does seem to be the case that I do not understand."

"You do not understand."

There was silence for a time, broken only by the foojy sound of our spoons.

"What I mean is, the idea is the idea, and my brother is my brother. There is no point in trying to change him. My father does not see, and it is so simple."

There was another silence, similarly punctuated.

"Will you give my brother a job?" She looked up resolutely.

I muttered something, and we reached bottom, and went our ways.

I have not hidden from you the fact that I am finding her useful in matters I seek to pursue. My conscience is not quiet; but how can I possibly explain to the paper my employing a pinball jockey whom I have not met and of whom everything I have heard suggests unemployability?

My own experience of the intellies informs me that your conclusions about the Choopies are not likely to be in error. Persons who come to Japan in search of the fresh and original should not seek it in the realm of ideas. I do not say that persons should be bent upon that search. I only say that they who are should look in the right place.

I will stay here for the better part of the week, even though I have already learned everything I am likely to learn about the martyrs. I want to investigate Korean successes in studying Japanese methods of selling our seats out from under us. Doubtless I will go on enjoying myself, and feeling guilty.

And how is Tokyo, as the Time of the Stirring of Bugs gives way to Midspring?

28. Miss Gray to Mr. Brown

In the ancient battle between adherents of spring and those of autumn, I do not know which side I am on. In the battle between the cherry and the dandelion, I am on the side of the latter. Such a cheerful little creature, so sturdy and uncomplaining, like a happy farmer. If you reply that it is very well when in bloom but untidy afterwards, I reply that it is so too with the cherry tree. A cherry tree after it has shed its blossoms looks sort of half chewed.

> When in bloom, so very happy,
> And when not, well, somewhat shabby.

A dandelion takes care of itself, and asks nothing, except your lawn. It is a better symbol of the Japanese than is the cherry.

I had a mixed time in Tokyo. My interviews with Women of Tomorrow were not rewarding.

The following is the conclusion to my last interview with Miss Kurozora:

"I hope that you will come and see us again, and let us benefit from your wisdom. I dislike the American government and all its policies, as do liberal progressive democratic persons the world over, but I like Americans."

74

"I would have been much happier if you had said the reverse."

Which I think left the honors with me.

She sees us, as distinguished from our malevolent government, as a nation of happy farmers. A nation of dandelions. The figure comes to me as I look down on the dandelions which do so well under my eaves, and which I will not let the gardener touch. I will tell him that they are our national flower, and sacred.

My stay with the Shiraito family was pleasant and interesting. The house is a large one, and it rambles and meanders, here all airily in the Japanese manner, there all stuffily in the Western. It is as well that I was given the sister's room, in the latter manner. Spring has not yet really come, although the calendar tells us that it is more than half over, and the former manner is chilly.

Of the inhabitants of the house, the mynah bird is the most amusing. It speaks English with a Japanese accent: "I'm a mynah bird," much as it might say "I'm a minor bard" were its accent the Queen's.

The father is the most interesting, and the second most amusing, by a short distance only. He took me into his study on the night I arrived. It is a most marvelous clutter of Chinese gimcrackery and scribbling.

I murmured apologies for having come in time of crisis.

"We would never have guests if we turned them away because of crises."

"But this must be an unusual sort of crisis. You must be worried about your daughter."

"Oh, it has happened to several of my classmates. It seems to be something about the times. They go underground, and then they come up again, and which is worse? But you have chosen the best of my daughters to be friends with. I am sure you sometimes wish, as I do, that she would go away, but she will do no harm."

"She says nice things about you too."

"When she writes to editors she calls me a war criminal. I am sure you have seen some of her letters to editors. She does not hide her light."

"It is her Chairman Mao thing. It will pass."

"Let us talk about China. Tell me about China."

We did for a time. He listened sadly to my description of the New Peking.

"You know, in the matter of Chairman Mao, I do not disagree as much with your friend my daughter as she thinks I do. I feel about him rather as I do about her: I can see the worth of him and the worth of her, only I wish they would go away sometimes. The Chinese needed him, but not so much of him. I have nightmares about how it would have been if we had been unable to rid ourselves of General and Mrs. MacArthur, and Mrs. Vining. I hope your friend Mr. Brown will not be persuaded to give my son work."

Startled, I asked how he knew about that.

"So she *did* ask Mr. Brown to give him work. I was sure she would."

"Well, I do not actually know that she did." And indeed I did not, then, though your Korean letter has confirmed what I anticipated. My disclaimer was lame, however, and late.

"I was sure she would. You must tell Mr. Brown not to. Do you play pinball?"

"Like a granny. I never win anything. Though some of the grannies around me do very well indeed. And when do you expect your youngest daughter to emerge above ground?"

"Oh, fairly soon, if she stays in the country and does not get into the newspapers and become famous. If she leaves the country we may never see her again at all. If she becomes famous she will have something to lose and stay under for a while. There are worse ways of becoming famous. She might have become a television talent. Why did you Americans have to give us television? Was democracy not enough?"

I did not see much of the "younger older brother," whom it is proposed that you hire. When I did see him, at breakfast, he was silent. He did not glower, exactly, but he seldom looked up. I said as we were putting on our shoes one morning that you were eager to meet him. You must forgive me, but I thought it might produce a response.

It did. "Ho, ho," he said, getting into his shoes more quickly than I and going out a few steps ahead of me.

I like his shaven head. It is blue-black, iridescent, halcyon-like.

The mother spent her time conjugating the verb "to be," most ingeniously, on several honorific levels. I was reminded of your touching lyric about the vernacular, composed on the eve of our birthday.

To hear Miss S. talk, I would have expected anger at the tyrannical ways of the father and an extra measure of affection for the mother as fellow victim and protector. I did not sense anything of the sort. Miss S.'s descriptive fragments, are, I suspect, conventional.

> On a mom
> One may qualm-
> > Lessly dote.
> On a pop
> It is prop-
> > Er to not.

The generation gap may be one of the things which the Japanese must have in greater measure than the rest of us, lest they be charged with imitation; but of which in fact their imitation is a pale one. For the real thing, come with me to Redrock.

There is another gap, of which our Miss Shiraito had told me nothing. Doubtless the silence informs us that it is nearer the real thing than the other.

The sister-in-law invited me to tea, out in the garden cottage. Miss Shiraito's expression, when she came home and heard of the invitation, said: "Well I never'" No words were spoken, but it seemed clear that no one in the family is ever invited out to the garden cottage.

Such a place of modern conveniences you never saw, shredders and blenders and wetters and driers and shrinkers and expanders, and extension cords like a school of octopi; and the baby was asleep in a closet, where there was a clear space. It had no cause to feel neglected, for there was a six-foot shelf on the making of children the modern way.

"We are in so many regards second to you Americans. We must try harder."

"But such ingenuity, I doubt that we could find the likes of it anywhere the world over. Just look if you will at this carpet shampooer. Do you have carpets?"

"Saturdays."

"And this electric corkscrew, and this noiseless alarm clock. (Whatever does it do to you?)"

"It must be a surprise to see me so near my mother-in-law. When you marry an oldest son and there are no homes for senior citizens, it happens. We must try harder."

"I live in a huddle with all my mothers-in-law."

It was too clever; but she was not listening. I wondered whether she was among (v.s.) "my daughters."

Here I am back in Kyoto, having taken a Radiant Express yesterday afternoon.

It is a good time of the year, as the day starts becoming longer than the night, and proceeds to become more so. What do you do with your spring evenings? Prune?

I will not be going to Tokyo again until just before my departure, for which I begin to prepare. I am trying to keep my rooms for another American, but my landlady is seeking a French lady, to bring international cultural exchange to higher levels than I have proved capable of. In a perverse moment I suggested that she seek a Korean or a Chinese, both of them representative of more venerable culture than a French lady, or, for that matter, my landlady herself.

"But I want a *foreigner*," she said.

And her eyes added: "Otherwise I would be a mere land-lady."

She is a dear.

29. Miss Gray to Miss Shiraito

You were very kind, and it was a great pleasure being with you and your family. Please thank all of them for me.

I keep asking myself what I might do in return. Gifts would somehow be formal and empty. Is the expression "coals to Newcastle" on your list of things? Everthing that is not made in Japan will be tomorrow, and so the prospect of surprising you with something new and exotic seems hopeless.

You must resolve my dilemma by coming to visit me. The cherries will soon be in bloom, and I will not be here so very much longer. You must take leave of Craft for a few days.

I have another reason for wishing you to come, and quickly. Down in the center of the city, I keep thinking I see your sister. More than once I have seen a young lady with exactly the fresh, round-faced prettiness of the picture on your desk.

It is the season which prompted a poet on your side of the water to exclaim:

There is something about a bed of violets!

On mine, in similar circumstances, a poet said:

I'll try and tell you what I mean.

I think we may here see the difference between the East and the West.

Do come and enjoy the season with me.

30. Miss Shiraito to Miss Gray

"Cloudy weather in springtime; a hazy sky in the flower season." So it is that my favorite dictionary defines the skies of the season, these sweet-sad days as springtime rises to a climax, so very fleeting, and goes into a decline. I doubt that in your native place there can be, in the light of the waning moon, this same delicate tracery of branch and mist. Yet it must have a quality all its own, a gibbous moon which sets to a howled accompaniment of coyotes and a whirred one of rattlesnakes.

Thank you for your letter. What you say of my sister certainly does interest me.

It gave me great pleasure to have from you indications that from your stay with us pleasure was not wholly absent. I hope I am not deceiving myself when I take your expressions of satisfaction to be sincere. The words themselves bring pleasure, and if sincerity may be read into them, the pleasure is more than quadrupled.

We all enjoyed having you. My father spoke of the enjoyment just yesterday at breakfast.

"A pity," he said, "that your Miss Gray did not stay a little longer. We could have had a good laugh over it."

My brother was also present, but upon such occasions it is one or another of us women who must perform as foil for my father.

"A good laugh over what?" said I.

"Over my favorite anniversary."

"Your favorite anniversary?" said my mother, though I am sure we had both remembered. It is a routine we have gone through for a number of years.

"On this April Fool's Day, almost twenty years ago now, the Anti-Prostitution Law went (in theory) into effect. We are told that Japanese intellectual and political life is wanting in humor, but there was *one* prime minister who had a sense of humor. A pity your Miss Gray is too new to these parts to have seen him in action."

"Oh but she has read so many books," said my mother.

We just cannot, you see, get over talking about you.

"Would you rather not have anti-prostitution?" asked I, in protest.

"Indeed, indeed I would."

"Miss Kurozora would like to meet you. She would like to tell you a thing or two."

"Your Miss Gray, now, is the sort of feminist I like. Miss

What's-her-name is all words. When we Japanese start giving in to words we are such silly people."

"It is a contradiction."

"It is a contradiction. I must tell Chairman Mao when next we meet."

"With your record?"

"But I think I might enjoy myself more in the land of your Miss Gray."

"I am going there myself," said my brother, quietly, suddenly. "I am going to America."

My father had worked his way back to the front page of the *Morning Flush*. He usually finds the front page (who does not?) worth no more than a glance, but this time he went over it diagonally, and then the reverse. His eye was at about the crossing of the diagonals when he said: "Tcha!"

He put aside the Flush and arose from the table. "I am glad I have two sons. One of them could, if I chose, be considered accidental, and dismissed. I do not choose to do so, quite yet."

"What is the opposite of accidental?" said my brother. "Inevitable?"

"Just let me look," said I, taking a dictionary of antonyms from my Boston bag, and hoping to get over the moment.

"What needs to be said is only this: I do not choose quite yet to dismiss you as worthless. There is all the difference in this world between your going to America and my going. I have no intention of going, although people tell me that the Bicentennial is going to be the funniest thing. There is all the difference in this world and several others."

The religious implications interested me, briefly; but I dismissed them. My brother said: "Tcha'" My mother had started for the garden when my brother entered the conversation.

"Do you have the money?" I asked, when my father had left the room.

"It all depends on what he meant by the clause following the colon."

"You flatter it by assigning it a meaning?"

"I have had a contingent offer of money."

"From your mother."

". . . ."

"And what is this contingency?"

"I have told you that some people, among them her, find him strangely but powerfully persuasive. That is why I assign to the clause in question a tentative meaning."

And that was our breakfast.

I tell you of it because I am writing, and because you may be seeing my brother in your land, America. Do you remember my telling you of a certain small request I had made of Mr. Brown, in my brother's behalf, on the train down-town? Has he spoken to you of it?

There beside a sunny wall, a cherry comes into bloom. The sun is over the garden of my eastern neighbor, and the moon over that of my western; and the cherry is in and out of a haze, or a mist, or something between.

> Oh be not sad, nor heave a sigh,
> Oh cherry blossom dear!
> I love to have thee here near by,
> And hope that thou dost not feel drear,
> Albeit that a haze now hides
> All aspect of thy top and sides,
> And likewise of thy rear.

I have here joined together two poems from one of our early anthologies. I sometimes think that the failure of our poetry to appeal to the alien sensibility has to do with its brevity, and that it why I take the liberty. What do you think?

Yes, I *will* go and visit you. I have just this moment decided. Please give my regards to your landlady, and my regrets that we must pass as ships in the night; and do not come down with anything.

31. Miss Shiraito to Mr. Brown

In all the hills, as the Radiant Express rushed by, was the radiance of spring. Yellow is the color of spring. As one pulls away from the pollution of the city there are patches and dots of yellow, daffodils and forsythia and rape, and more and more, and yet more and yet more. Then there is a falling off as pollution takes over again, and yellow and pollution in rhythmic alternation, and one is in Kyoto. So it is, on a Radiant Express, on a day in April.

I enclose thirteen polaroids, of me and that number of famous cherry trees, not as considerable a number as I would have wished.

My round of the famous cherry trees has been less than exhaustive because I have been streetwalking. Mostly I have been walking a riverside block recommended by Professor Gray, where she says that eventually I will meet everyone. I was about to give up, telling myself that she had it confused with Ginza, when today it happened: making my way northwards, I saw a familiar pair of jeans, also proceeding northwards.

I darted around the block clockwise, making no attempt to apologize as I ricocheted from person to person. It is better not to apologize at all if one does not have time to do it properly; and it was raining.

Out once again on the riverside street, I now slowed my pace and headed southwards. I sought to look nonchalant, and to keep out of sight, behind a large foreigner.

He turned and smiled grinningly. "If you cannot beat us," he said, "join us," and he laughed what I think may have been a horselaugh, a sort to attract attention, in any event, whatever the proper word for it may be.

It was enough to attract the attention of the whole block, my sister as well. She bolted.

"Stop them!" I said somewhat peremptorily to the American as I sped off after my sister. I thought the laugh American, and I was right, as presently it obtained.

Three of them, all in blue jeans, had been side by side, my

sister and two men. They (the men) had beards. When my sister commenced bolting, they did not do likewise. It was in their regard that I left instructions with the American.

Shrilling all the while, I followed my sister across the river and into a railway station, where, ticketless, she boarded a southbound train. I too attempted to board, but a door came between us.

Having conveyed sincere sorrow at my want of a ticket, I was allowed to pass back through the wicket, and returned to the west bank of the river, where I discovered that an amusing thing had happened. A policeman had come up, and was detaining not the bearded jeans but the American. The latter was not making himself understood terribly well. I joined the crowd of onlookers and, with them, enjoyed it all for a time. It was very amusing.

"May I be of service?" I said presently, stepping forward.

"Well, yes, by Jesus, you may." (And I had thought him Jewish!) "Who do you think got me into this?"

I smiled prettily, unable to answer, having been off across the river when it was happening. I believe he had recognized me. So had others.

"It is this young lady towards whom his lewdness was directed," said a lady with an Osaka accent. It seemed a pity that the foreigner could not enjoy the comedy with me. But the day is coming. I am sure it is. That is what international cultural exchange is about.

"What sort of lewdness was he guilty of?" said the policeman.

"Well, tell him what happened," said the American.

"I do not know. I cannot say."

"Great Moses and the lifeguards'" And so I was in doubt once more as to whether he was Christian or Jewish.

Well, that was how it started, and we got to be rather good friends before the afternoon was over, and certainly that was very nice.

A police car came up and we were invited inside.

"Lewd foreigner here," said the policeman, as if asking the assent of the crowd, which it nodded.

The American demurred in the matter of entering the police car.

"Where are we going?"

"To the station."

"Why?"

"So that you can explain everything. So that you can apologize."

"Well Jesus Christ and the chickens got loose!"

"Are you a Christian?"

The way he looked at me! How terrible, I thought, if the wrath of America were ever again directed at our poor little country. I do not in the least mind being asked whether I am a Buddhist, but I should have remembered that you Americans take these things more seriously.

On the way to the station I sought to distract him from his imagined troubles. I asked whether he liked the Kabuki drama, and the tea ceremony, and how he felt about the atom bomb, and about Japanese women.

"I have never seen one," he kept replying.

I was about to ask whether he had problems with his vision, but we had arrived at the station.

And all the while my sister was being borne southwards towards Osaka. Poor thing!

"And do you like Bugaku?" said I as we entered the station. His apprehension seemed to be mounting to ludicrous heights.

"Oh bugger Bugaku!" is I think what he said, though I am not sure, and such dictionaries as I have with me do not help.

"They will merely ask for an apology," said I, as we went up the stairs.

"They will not get one. Show me a more innocent bystander. Go ahead, show me one."

"Things are never simple, and there is no point in pretending that they are. So much has happened since Commodore Matthew Calbraith Perry, U.S.N., came, which would not otherwise have happened." Seeing the expression on his face, I quickly changed the subject. "Do you like geisha girls?"

I was determined to say nothing to the police. In my mind,

however, was forming a poem.

> Excuse me, please. I beg your pardon.
> My father went to kindergarten.

Etc. I wonder what those provincial police would have said had they known that they had before them someone whose father was in a certain kindergarten of Sendai with an assistant chief of the Tokyo Metropolitan Police. But I said nothing.

"Now if you will just sign an apology," said I, giving the gist of what the policeman had said at the counter at some length.

"Why don't *you* have to sign an apology?"

"This is Japan," said I.

Meanwhile the policeman at the counter seemed to have difficulty finding the apology form for lewdness.

"I am reminded," said the American, apparently in improved spirits, "of the time I was accused of opening a bank account."

"What possessed you?"

"But it was all right. I had only turned in the application forms, and not yet done anything serious. What is this?"

"An apology. Just something for the file."

"An apology for what?"

Glancing at it, I saw that it was an apology for perjury. Since I did not at the time know the English for perjury, I could do little to explain.

"It would be better to obey," said I. "Just something for the file."

"Our only desire," said the policeman at the counter, "is to make your stay a pleasant one."

"How do you feel about *wabi* and *sabi*?" said I, for nameless agitation seemed to be mounting once more.

"I just adore them," he said, and signed.

The original policeman, now quite frolicsome, stopped a cab for us and saw us into it. The American took the little police paw in his great hairy American one and shook it mightily.

"I too hope that my stay in Japan will be a pleasant one," he said. "I hope, further, that you will be modest and prudent and guard against arrogance and impetuosity, and assure you that I

86

for my part will be imbued with a spirit of self-criticism and have the courage to correct mistakes and shortcomings." And he blew a kiss, uselessly, I am inclined to think, since few people in the provinces are sufficiently cosmopolitan to recognize the significance of such a gesture.

"*C'est la vie*," said I, "Mr. – I am not entirely sure that I caught your name."

"Rooby. Mr. Rooby is my name." And he sang a little song somewhat *sotto voce*, to the tune of "America the Beautiful":

> In *wabi* land, in *sabi* land,
>   One can yet find some peace,
> And quietly disturb it and
>   Enliven the police.

"I think that when I get back to my native place I will join the *wabi-sabi* lobby. I used to think that the Korea lobby was the best thing going, but I think that I have changed my mind. Thank you for this lovely afternoon. But for you I might have gone through life without a police record."

"What about the bank account?"

"I had only turned in the *forms*. How often do I have to tell you?"

Back in the city, we had French Licks at a very poor Kyoto imitation of Fuji House. I learned – what a day it has been for chance fortuities! – that he is a friend of Mr. Gold's. Is that not interesting?

Professor Gray is at one of those rallies. She goes to a great many.

It is a dark, moonless night, of a sort when dreams go flitting by. Let me give you a dream poem or two, from one of the anthologies I seem to have with me.

There is this one:

> Since I saw my dear in a nap,
> I've known a dream is a sweet hap.

And there is this one:

> Whene'er my yearnings grow strong and stout,
> I put on my night gown inside out.

The poetess is a very famous one, and so is the translator. The second one may puzzle you.

Outside my window a peach tree is shedding its blossoms. It was under full-blown peach trees that the Doll Festival took place before Commodore Perry came.

Do you think that my sister is all right, down in Osaka? (Poor thing!)

Professor Gray says that she is sure that you like ginkgo trees. I am glad.

32. Miss Shiraito to Miss Gray

The moon of the Third Day was just setting as I made my way back to these western marches of Tokyo. I tried to think of it as an old moon, not a new, for in the decline would be fit symbol of my dejection upon returning from the Ancient Capital and the most pleasant time I had with you.

Thank you very much indeed. The colors in the hills, as I sat on the Radiant Express, were in keeping with my sense of the passing of a happy time. The splashes of faint pink upon my westward journey had sunk back once more into the varied greens. The peach blossoms have fallen, as have the single-petaled cherry blossoms, and it is still too early for the double.

> Oh can you tell me, do you know.
> Where is the dwelling of the gust
> That blows the blossoms into dust?
> For if you can, then I will go,
> And lodge a firm complaint, I trow.

Of the poems in the anthologies I had at hand, this one says it best.

If you should come upon my sister again, now that you know it is she, please point her in the right direction. Although my mother wants me to go to Sendai for Golden Week (about that more in a moment), I could go again to Kyoto if I thought it would be of use. You will by then have departed, of course, and the Basque lady will have moved in, and I have forgotten almost all the Basque I ever knew.

In the mail which awaited me on my return was an unsigned card. You can help me, I think, since it is somewhat in English. It is typed, save for the question mark, which is penned in. There is no signature.

> Are we not to sing, oh,
> To the merry ginkg-oh,
> Found malingering
> 'Neath the badger thing?
> Badger thing and ginkg-oh,
> Hey and ding-a-ding, oh!

I know whom it is from, despite the absence of a signature. That is not the problem. Mr. Brown's typewriter has no question mark. The absence of it is to keep him from temptation, he says. His newspaper does not like question marks. No, the problem is what the tone of the poem suggests about his acceptance of and intentions toward the potted ginkgo which I left with his watchman. I have tried to call him, but without success.

Well what do you know! I just tried again, and made an interesting discovery! If you ring thrice and then hang up and then ring again, Mr. Brown will answer with great alacrity! I made the discovery quite by accident. I had come to the third ring when there was a screaming in the kitchen. I hung up, not because the screaming alarmed me, but because I was afraid it might alarm him. The explanation is always the same: the mynah bird has let something escape. This time it was a cockroach. The screaming did not last long. It seldom does. I rang again, and there was Mr. Brown, quicker than you could say: "Now here is an interesting discovery!"

I have tried several times now, and each time it has worked: ring three times, and hang up, and commence ringing again.

The night is very dark and very clear, but there are no stars. I went out a little while ago and did my duty as a citizen, and I trust that if my fellow citizens did as well, Governor Minobe will have the mandate he needs to bring back stars. My father and brother are both out. The mynah bird seems to have created enough stir for one day, and quiet reigns in that quarter as well. In the matter of my sister I have had one more thought: if you do come upon her, and she wants to go to America with you, that will be all right, I am sure. No one will be inconvenienced. There might be disagreement were the case that of my brother.

"Has anything happened?" I asked my mother as, upon my return from Kyoto, I hoisted my book bag from my shoulder. It is a routine question.

"Your grandmother may come from Sendai."

"How nice. Why?"

"For Golden Week, and your younger older brother." Of whom, you will remember, my mother is not the mother.

"How nice. Why?"

"I told her you were going to Sendai for Golden Week. You are, I think?"

"I thought I might go to Kyoto again."

"I think you should both go to Sendai. If you do not your grandmother will come here."

We will see. It were better, perhaps, not to tell the Basque lady to expect me.

The election returns are beginning to come in. The indications are that the people have spoken. Good for them.

The peach blossoms now having fallen, *Kerria japonica*, sometimes called "yellow rose," which it is not at all, come into a cascade of golden bloom. Do I but imagine that it is golden even in this Third Night's darkness?

33. Miss Shiraito to Mr. Brown

Azaleas bloom, and we are on the verge of the Time of the Grain Rains, the last fortnight of spring, when rains are hoped for, towards grains. Some years we get more (rain) than hoped for, and this seems to be one of them. "*Sho, sho, sho, sho, sho,*" falls the rain. "*Pota, pota, pota, pota, pota,*" it falls. One evening in Cosmopolitan Culture House a wise man remarked that the absence of such palpable words makes English inadequate as a vehicle for Zen. I think that it is true.

> Nightly cry the frogs
> In all the paddy bogs.
> And whence came so much water?
> From a Shiraito daughter
> Weeping *pota, pota, pota.*

It is a stance which I have borrowed from a famous poet of old, and made my own. It has the double merit of according with this gloomy night of spring rains, and requiring that my name be pronounced correctly, four distinct syllables and no diphthongs, such as not even you accord it, after all this time.

I long to have your views on the recent elections, and feel sure that you will call me one day soon.

I am worried about my brother, and do not know what to make of the silence which has been in uninterrupted attendance upon the query which I made of you in his regard. The chief difference between my brother and my sister, aside from surface differences, is that my father also seems to worry about my brother. Would that it were not so, but it is. When may I expect an answer to my query?

My brother and I are going to Sendai for Golden Week. There we will beard my grandmother, who might otherwise come to Tokyo and join forces with my father.

"Breakfast has become such a lonely affair," said my father as he took up the *Flush* this morning, and only my mother and I to bear witness. "I must take steps to reverse the process of attrition. I may say that I have some confidence in their being successful. Well, well. That Miss Shiraito has been writing letters again. She says that the people have spoken, and what they have said is: 'Harmony.' A maiden so shut off from the winds that blow (eastern? western?) is a rare thing these days. I really do wish that you would look her up and bring her to tea."

"Who, sir, could disagree?"

But it was his second sentence that weighed heavily, and seemed fraught.

I went yesterday with Mr. Rooby to Fuji House – you remember Mr. Rooby, him of the amusing little Kyoto mixup.

"Thank you for your kind assistance the other day," he said, after we had had a few moments with our Joies de Chicago.

"Not at all," said I, diffidently. "I only hope that it added to the pleasure of your stay in our Ancient (from 794) Capital."

"So now I am free until I again commit – what was it?"

"Perjury," said I, having brushed up. "If you think you need help, perhaps I can put one of our Craft lawyers at your service. My father says that they keep us out of trouble which we richly deserve. It is the sort of thing he says."

There followed another silence. Our spoons had become mired.

"And will they be able to keep you free of good old Harry Gold and his contrivances, and the fact that his home office might just possibly spill a few peanuts, almost any day now?"

"I am sure," said I, somewhat haughtily, it may have been, "that our executives know how to manage foreign unpleasantness. They have all of them lived for protracted periods in your native city."

But I was interested, chiefly because of you. "Mr. Brown," said I to myself upon taking cognizance of his last sentence. "Mr. Brown will want to fly back to Los Angeles for the spilled peanuts. I will miss him."

I was sorry that you were not at home when I wandered by last night. I trust that the doorman delivered the pruning hooks, and the copies, as well, of *Prune!* and the sequel, *Prune!!*, perhaps an even better guide to the subject. Your ginkgo will require pruning, and I think that it probably needs a mate as well.

I see you in my mind's eye, jogging pinkly around the lake. Do not, I pray you, overdo it. The advent of summer is but a fortnight away, and temperatures rise and pulse as well, with "summer defeat," the symptoms of which are sweating and gasping. Think of the loss to the world were we to find you in this condition!

34. Miss Shiraito to Miss Gray

We are on the eve of the Time of the Grain Rains. The rain drips from the boughs and the eaves and drips yet more, *pota, pota, pota, pota, pota*. Outside my window an azalea is like an *ignis fatuus* in the marsh which the garden has become, and the willow threads are strands of jade as they move in and out of the light.

> On the willow sparkles the dew.
> "And how many years have passed over you?"

I must explain – so often one must when translating poetry. The question is addressed not to you, Professor Gray, but to the willow.

I write in a great hurry, barely pausing for the amenities. Mr. Brown has told me not to call him, and so I have not had the word which you said you would relay through him of your departure, which must be eminent. I want very much to see you when you pass through Tokyo, and I have in the meantime a small favor to ask of you.

Yesterday I attended our fortnightly class reunion at White Lily. Just inside the gate there was a cluster of persons, helmeted and teatoweled, and armed with staves, chains, whips, collapsible lead pipes, etc., doubtless awaiting a rival bund.

A thought came to me, quite on the moment.

"My mother is dying," I said. "Where is my sister?" I brought a sleeve to my eyes, sobbed convulsively for a time, and wrung the sleeve out. It was a Japanese sleeve.

Observing that the effect was as I would have wished, I commenced sobbing once more.

"Who might the person be by whom one is addressed?" shrilled one of them.

Yes, it was an oversight. "Yoko de Shiraito," I replied, gaspingly.

It was a fib. My mother has not been dying at all. Just a few moments ago I saw her down in the garden, collecting creatures for the mynah bird.

The line of helmets and tea towels became a circle. There did not seem to be a consensus. The conference continued. I continued, though beginning to ache, to sob.

A helmet came forward. "The Ancient (from 794) Capital. We believe her to be down by the River Kamo in that city. We are sorry about your mother, and hope that she is well."

You will have guessed the favor I must ask of you. Could you spend some time loitering by the river, in the part of the city in which my own loitering proved so successful? Perhaps you could take your packing with you. You will remember her rotund visage, I am sure.

"Thank you," said I.

"Poor thing," said they. I do not know whether they meant me, or my sister, poor thing, down in Kyoto, or my mother, in whose regard they had already offered commiserations.

I am aware of a certain urgency as tokens of summer come forth. Time is short. There is always your Basque successor, of course – but I feel more at home, somehow, with the American spirit of dissension.

You are wise to leave Kyoto before the advent of summer. I hope that I never have to go down and find out for myself.

94

35. Mr. Brown to Miss Gray

The Moon of the Thirteenth Night is high. It seems to be associated with wistful, autumnal things. At this most florid of seasons, when the double cherries are with us and the peonies and the azaleas and the wistaria are about to burst upon us, the image is doubtless misplaced. Yet it does not seem so at all. I am wistful.

> The lunar orb, this Thirteenth Night,
>   Rose cheerless over Hilda Gray.
> There came a voice: "Take fright, take fright!"
>   And Hilda Gray she went away,
> And we are left to face the day
>   That brings a lonely Fourteenth Night,
> And after that the cheerless day
>   That brings a joyless Fifteenth Night,
> And after that . . .

When the lyrical flow gets started, you have a time stopping it.

I will miss you. We have not seen a great deal of each other, but it has been good to know that there is someone down there with whom I can have exchanges.

I almost thought, so high were your spirits, that you were glad to be leaving. I was glad for them, and wistful. I had feared, from what you said over the telephone about your reluctance to become further involved with Miss Shiraito's sister, that Miss Shiraito herself might not be at the airport; but there she was, along with all those others.

Quite a gathering it was, too. Wherever did all those picture-snappers come from? Did each of your leatherstocking friends bring her own? What brutes of people they are (the snappers I mean, although the leatherstockings are somewhat that way too), climbing on tables, crawling under tables, knocking tables over.

Miss S. and I took the monorail back into town together. There were leatherstockings and snappers aboard, and she seemed drawn to them. She remained steadfastly at my side, however.

"She was a good friend," she said, of you, looking out over the filled-in wastes through which the monorail makes its way from the airport. "But she said nothing of my sister."

"Maybe she did, and was drowned out." It may have been too jocular, but I did not want the conversation to move on to her brother.

"I enjoyed walking that street beside the river. It was all I did enjoy. Everywhere else reminded me of how we went there in busses and vomited, in the third grade. I thought she might enjoy it too. But she was a good friend."

"You must remember that it is a risky business for her. I can plead the privilege of the press, but she cannot."

We had come to the race track. If I were a writer of letters to editors, I would ask why bays need be filled in to provide land for race tracks. The dandelions were fine, however. The arc lights had them half open.

"It is all right. I do not worry about my sister. It is strange, because she is probably in the most danger."

I was glad that solid old ground had come beneath us once more, and the end of the journey was near.

"I wish you could hear what my father is always saying about American companies. If he had not worked harder than that when he was in China, he would have 'died in a ditch' (Kenkyusha). He is not always saying it. He said it at breakfast one morning when my brother was there. He said even worse things about Japanese who work in American companies. Why?"

"Well, on the whole, I think he is right."

"My brother would not work in a Japanese company."

"A pivot word" And this pleasantry saw us through to the terminus.

"I will think of larger things. I will think of the day of Professor Gray's return, and the support she will be lending us in the meantime, far away."

I am *sure* we will have the support of Miss G.,
Far away over the sea though she be.

And further:

> Oh see you the hand of Miss G.,
> Extended far over the sea,
> To offer a grip
> Of amityship
> And choopified sorority?

We parted. I had to look into certain details of the approaching visit of the Korean prime minister, that the people of Los Angeles may know; and in any event Foojy House closes early. It takes a long time to clean up.

Has spring yet come to your high plains? Do write and let me know.

36. Miss Shiraito to Mr. Brown

Had we not rain, it would be a night refulgent with moonlight. For it is the night of the full moon. I think I am glad that we have rain. The moon is left to the imagination. Here we have an important difference between the East and the West.

Hark! In the vernal darkness is a thing which has brought thoughts to generations and centuries of poets. Can you guess what it is?

> An owl, a water rail, a lark?
> Nay, none of these. A goose in the dark!

I enjoyed our ride in from the airport. Did you notice the tiny flower along the tracks, purple, I should judge, rendered more so by the brilliant illumination? I wished to call it to your attention, and query you as to its identity, but you were just then gazing meditatively at something in the middle distance which seemed to accord with your mood. Yes, the bittersweet taste of parting is to be savored in silence, and in communion with the grasses along the way.

I keep wondering how I would get through to you if something were to be crucial. Your aversion to telephones seems excessive, but I respect it.

Well for goodness sake! You have two telephones! Information has just informed me of that fact. They both seem to be busy. Are you being bothered by more than one person? Why *will* you not hire a detective?

I wandered down to the library today, thinking you might be there at the *Wall Street Journal.* Instead I found Mr. Rooby. We went to the coffee shop in the Monstrous Bank, across the street, and had each of us a cup of American coffee.

"Let us talk about crime," he said presently. "I have been thinking about it a great deal."

"Oh, you shouldn't. It was just something for the files."

"I don't mean my personal crime. I stopped pitying myself some time ago. I mean crime in general. I have been thinking about it. So has old Harry."

Mr. Gold, you will remember, in whom you are so much more interested than in most Americans.

"Harry thinks that perjury is taken more seriously on the far side of the ocean than on this. He says that here we have a difference between the East and the West."

"Numbers of us have remarked upon the difference."

"You ask someone a question under oath over there on the other side, says Harry, not that he has ever done it himself, and you are likely to get an honest answer. Ask someone here, and flip a coin, he says. He thinks there may soon be some honest answers over there. Maybe one of these days we will not be seeing each other for a while, he says."

We had a leisurely conversation, because at the price you pay for coffee it takes time to get your money's worth. I give you the part that I think will interest you.

It is the sort of thing I might want to discuss over the telephone, were that route permitted me.

98

Also, I might want to talk of my brother.

I hear proud talk of brothers at White Lily reunions.

"My brother is being sent to London. I am so glad it is not New York, because he likes to speak English."

"My brother is being sent to Paris. I am so glad it is not New York, because he likes culture."

"My brother is being sent to Hamburg. I am so glad it is not New York, because he likes Beethoven."

And what am I to say? That my own brother is jangling away in the Cosa Nostra Pinball Parlor, and shows no will to do anything else for the rest of his life? And when they start talking about bonuses, for the bonus season will soon be at hand, and whether they who manufacture do better than they who are in trade, and whether, among these last, they who must meet the demanding standards of the domestic market do better than they who sell abroad – am I to say that my brother's take of cigarettes and chocolate averages much the same, despite slumps, from month to month, and despite the fact that there may occasionally be something novel when Cosa Nostra takes over a bankruptcy? Am I to say these things? I but smile, hoping that they will be consumed with curiosity, and a sense of mystery and depth. They know that my father has Chinese connections.

My brother was at breakfast yesterday and again today.

This morning after breakfast I followed him to his room, which he keeps locked when he is not in the house. He does it to annoy. He knows that we could any one of us climb from the garden at any time he or she wished to, and get in through the closet.

"Do you take these things with you east of the river?" I asked, of the things he was putting into a small bag.

"Hitherto."

"Henceforth?"

"It may be that you will be seeing more of me on this side of the river."

"Because you do not want to go? Because she does not want you?"

"The latter is nearer."

My mother was at the door, without seeming to be. There was in the manner of both of us something to suggest that we did not wish it to seem that we noticed.

"The latter is nearer, though not quite it."

"Oh." I do not think that a question mark is needed, though I sought to convey a delicate element of query.

"There was an article in the *Flush* the other morning about black spots. A black spot is what is left behind when a star collapses. It is there, but cannot be observed, except by its effects on other bodies."

My mother's step as she moved on said that she did not care whether it seemed to us that she did not seem to be there or not.

"Oh?" The note of inquiry was stronger this time.

"There is a black spot, off to one side, or to the rear. It is not really that she does not want me; but this black spot has an effect."

I needed no explanation, but you are an American. He meant Father.

"You have not forgotten, I know, that we go to Sendai for Golden Week," I called after him as he strode from the room and into his shoes.

I view our journey to Sendai, over Golden Week, as something that must be. No one, save possibly my sister in Sendai, wants my grandmother to come here.

We laugh at her Sendai accent. We are like a television audience, prepared to laugh at anything and nothing. Were she to say, "I am suffering from a terminal ailment, my dears, and must die a week from Saturday," we would laugh heartily. Yet she requires being listened to.

Now the full moon of the Third Month, rising towards zenith, breaks through the clouds, and we have an Ugetsu, a night of rainy moonlight. Lovely it is, too, the Ugetsu, catching dewdrops on the foliage, turning them to tiny lightlets.

> And doth't, this lovely Ugetsu,
> As't doth to me, bring thoughts to you,

Of things, including Hilda Gray,
Over the seas and far away?

I wonder where my sister is tonight.

37. Miss Gray to Mr. Brown

It is the time of year when Redrock is least like Tokyo. There you have all the things of spring. Here it is still winter, harsh, windswept winter. A waning moon hangs in a sky of an almost blinding blue; and the winds blow, and blow. It has been a dry winter. The plains are endlessly brown and yellow. Yet spring does seem to be approaching. There is wonder in the thought that pasqueflower and columbine will shortly bloom upon these windswept plains.

Let me set you a verbal puzzle. Miss Shiraito tells me that you are fond of them. Find, if you will, the columbine in the following poem, from an early court anthology, rendered into English by a well-known translator of the land of its origin:

> The high and low both will once be
> At the height of their prosperity.

There is a columbine in the original, I do assure you. So often something gets lost, at the hands of the most skilled translator.

You told me not to write until I felt comfortable again. Well, that may take a while. And when I have comfortably settled down and am in harmony with things, it may be that acceptance will make itself known in ever more insistent complaining. It is what is done, here, and perhaps it is done because people enjoy it. I seem to detect mellowness, nostalgia, even, as if the constant talk of how one's neighbors are encroaching on one's property from all sides and the Feds are encroaching on everyone's were an afterglow of the wild frontier, not so very far away.

Complain, Ms. Gray, complain,
That you may again
Feel
Real
Uptight downright deep in the swing
Of things, and everything.

I think that we have more Orientals about than when I went away, though I cannot be sure. Our enrollment figures do not provide information about race. I think too that we have more street people. At lower milder altitudes spring has already come, and in their push towards the mountains, where they will summer, the street people are a bit ahead of it. So there they are shivering upon our sidewalks and in our creek bottoms.

Crossing the creek down behind the auditorium, I asked a question. The results were not satisfying.

"Are you Japanese?"

"No."

"But wasn't that Japanese you were speaking?"

"Yes."

"Then aren't you Japanese?"

"Yes."

"Why didn't you say so in the first place?"

"I did."

You will see what went wrong. It was only afterwards, back up on the hill, that I saw. One forgets how dangerous it is to ask negative questions, what confusion they can lead to.

It was good of you to come to the airport. I am sorry that the leatherlegged choopies and the blackheaded snappers so got in the way. I have not heard from Miss Shiraito and I have heard from you. You are the one from whom I would have expected remissness; but I am glad, both ways. I really do hope that I have no further part in the affairs of the younger Miss Shiraito.

Let me hear from you again. You know how good it is to have letters when you are feeling neither here nor there.

38. Miss Shiraito to Mr. Brown

Here in the north country the eaves are deep, as not in the city. I ask myself: how must it be among the heaped-up snows of winter? Then must one truly have the feel of the north country. (And indeed one does.) Spring is slow, here in the north. The zelkovas of Tokyo already take on that dark, sour hue of summer, while here they are a fresh yellow-green, the green of the beds of seedling rice, such a pleasure to the eye from the train window.

We had no choice but to make our journey today if we were to take advantage of Golden Week at all. There was the matter of the horoscope, and that of my brother's recalcitrance. He said on the Emperor's Birthday that he must go and sign the palace register. Of course there was no need for him to do any such thing. He only said it to annoy my father. He said it at breakfast, and if his intent was to annoy, he succeeded.

"That is the sort of thing your paternal grandmother might do," said my father, taking up the *Flush* with an indignant crackling noise. Though a feudal reactionary, my father is of the view that such things as palace registers only emphasize the decay. "Why this year, after all those others?"

"The august reign now extends over fifty calendar years."

"When people like you say things like that, I begin to doubt that there will be a fifty-first."

I do not for a moment think that my brother actually signed the register. A great multitude seems to have been at the palace gates, and if there is a thing he cannot abide it is a multitude. (Which is another reason why he would do better in a foreign company.) I wonder if he even knows the emperor's name. It is not, as you seem to think, Charlie. Because the matter is of so little import, I have not sought to disabuse you.

In any event, my brother and I made our way to Sendai on this day when I might have joined the Craft cell in demonstrating for peace, fraternity, and sorority. No doubt the streets of Tokyo were inundated with these things. Did you go out and observe, that you might report to the people of Los Angeles?

But a horoscope is a strange thing. Sometimes it seems to get out of hand. Today is a Day of Great Peace and a day of peace as well, and perhaps we should have been apprehensive of the coincidences. Perhaps we should have let my grandmother come to Tokyo. Then she (and not we) would have come bearing gifts, and my mother is a fusser over gifts, and time would have passed. My grandmother scarcely fusses at all.

We removed our wraps and offered our gifts, which she crammed into the altar, knocking over the cenotaph of my father's younger older brother.

"And do you have good news for me?"

So it began, without ado.

"Well, there is the news about Governor Minobe," said I, cheerfully, though I knew that the query was directed at my brother. My grandmother seldom directs a query at me when my brother is in sight.

"Yes, it is nice to see Tokyo getting what it deserves." I was pleased and flattered, I must confess, that she had taken notice of my little riposte. "But you know Governor Minobe has not been on my lists. I hear such peculiar things about him."

"Your lists of what?" said I, knowing full well.

Again she noticed me. "Of prospective daughters-in-law."

"Do you have lists, as well, of prospective sons-in-law?"

"Governor Minobe might do for you, as a matter of fact. Is he free at the moment? I had not much thought about it. You are so young."

Now my brother and I, as you know, are almost exactly the same age.

"Younger and younger, people say."

"I am sure they do. I must listen more carefully. So I am to conclude that you have brought me no good news? Let us turn then from the past and the present to the future."

"I like being in Sendai," said my brother at last, looking out over the garden. "It gives me a feeling that the past is longer than we had thought. That there is more time."

"More time for what?"

"Oh, for a nice long talk." He went down into the garden.

It is a beautiful one. It looks as if it had been left to itself for a very long time, and had chosen to do what a gardener might have forced it to do. I like it better, I think, than the famous gardens of Kyoto. It has that look of having made the best, and a very good best, of a not very good thing.

"All by yourself?"

"I mean to work yet awhile, and learn something of the world." To be civil, I pretended that her query had included me. "Have you thought how strange it is that our sex has known so little of the world for such a long time?"

"It is more important for boys to marry than for girls." There can be little doubt that her Sendai modulations carried to the far corners of the garden. "The two do of course go together. Leastways they used to in my day."

"I would have expected you to disagree with Father." I believe I may claim to have said it somewhat spiritedly.

"He uses the family argument. He says that we have always married in our family, and on the whole it has done the family good. I argue rather the selfish case of the individual. Do you suffer from cold feet, as your grandfather used to?" she asked my brother, who had returned to the veranda. "He used to say that he did not know what a warm foot was until he got married."

"Have any of them," said my brother, nodding toward the cenotaphs, "been dismissed from the circle for remaining bachelors?"

"There have been no bachelors in our family for generations and generations. For ever, I might say. There was a grand uncle of your father's who tried to kill himself and failed, the worst way. You will not find him there. You have replied to my question with a question of your own. That is not permitted."

"Well, yes, I do suffer from cold feet. There are other remedies."

"Oh, none as good. None a third as good. I used to remark to your grandfather: 'You polygamists do not see that men need women far more than women need men. Therefore it is wrong for one man to have several women. It means that some have

105

none.' I think he agreed with me, though he never put the doctrine into practice."

So the conversation kept coming back to marriage. I would far rather have had it dwell on suicide for a time.

"That is as it is in each heart," said I.

"Ha," said my brother.

"Ho," said my grandmother.

And I did not record what else was said.

The *Lespedeza bicolor* for which Sendai has been celebrated in song and poetry over the centuries is out of season. Were I to send you sprigs of something grandly in bloom, it would probably be *Kerria japonica*, for which Sendai is not famous at all, and besides my grandmother and I have had words about the enormous sprays with which she embowers the cenotaphs, and which I think were better left out in the environment.

> O Mistress of this *Kerria*, forget
> You not my brief injunction: *stet.*

I would tie my injunction to a twig, as poets have done from time immemorial; but my grandmother does not know Latin.

My brother and I will return on Monday, the end of Golden Week. It is a dismal day for returning. Golden Week usually manages to stretch itself by joining a weekend at one end or the other, but this year it does not. In this as in so many matters my grandmother has opinions. She says that the weekend is exactly where it ought to be, buried where no one will notice it. She says that the long weekend and Ms. Vining are the very worst things the Americans did to us. As regards Ms. Vining, my father agrees. He says that he looks forward to a victorious war at the end of which we will send a baroness to be tutor to your vice-president.

This Day of Great Peace will shortly give way to the Day of the Red Maw. Since we are off to such a bad start on the former, the latter does not bear thinking about. Yet I must confess that I like being here. There is a quiet repose about my grandmother's establishment, despite the overdone cenotaphs, which suggests changelessness, even as my grandmother

106

emerges as a cruel force demanding change. So it goes. Life is a paradox, or series of them.

There are frogs out in the fields, where the seedling rice waits quietly under a half moon, all unaware (or is it?) that it must soon be transplanted.

> Hark! There was a sound of water.
> An ancient pond, and plump!
> A salientian jump!

And what is it that you do under this same half moon? Slumber warmly, pinkly?

39. Miss Shiraito to Miss Gray

Here in the north country the eaves are deep, as not in the city. How must it be among the heaped-up snows of winter? Spring comes slowly to this north country. In Tokyo the zelkovas take on the dark hue of summer, while here they are a fresh yellow-green, the green of seedling paddy, so pleasant to view from the train window.

I must be brief. It is almost midnight, and I wish to set down at the end of my letter the date of this joyous people's day. To set it down after midnight would be fraudulent, and invite something.

All is still, save for frogs jumping into ancient ponds. A half moon turns the *Kerria japonica* to a cascade of silver. Are you similarly observing, at your midnight bower?

> Who else observing, at her bower,
> The ghostly cascade of the *kerria* flower
> Pulls herself up with a start and a thump?
> Into an old pond, a batrachian jump!

But no: over your high plains, if my conversion table be quite correct, the sun has risen some time since, upon this joyous people's day.

I scribble to apologize for my silence since your departure, to inquire after your health, and to convey my grandmother's greetings. She is glad that I am making American friends.

"They have so much to give," she said. "You must not let them know that you have anything at all to give in return. The mistakes of your father's generation are not the ones your generation accuses them of. The Americans would have gone on loving us if they had gone on thinking we had nothing to lose. But you are too young to understand. Just be quiet, and ever so friendly."

I must bring you to Sendai some time. You might not be able to enjoy her Sendai accent as it deserves, but you would be welcome, as you can see.

I have another reason for these scribblings. I must tell you of my sister's spoor, which we have picked up once more.

"Several of the boys in the bund were made note of at Haneda evening before last," said my mother, morning before last, when we were down in the garden gathering things.

"What bund?" asked I, innocently.

"Why the Latin-American Afro-Asian Mutual Self-Defense Popular Cooperative Bund. What other?"

"And when you say 'made note of,'" I asked further, hastening after a centipede, which I captured beneath a tree peony, "what is it that you mean?"

This was her account.

My father's friend the assistant chief of police keeps my father informed. I wonder if he would not be as happy were my sister to stay forever a hop, skip, and jump ahead of the police. On the evening averted to by my mother, a police ear was caught, as it probed the customs gate, by a peculiar style of incantation. From the certain remove at which the ear was, the incantation sounded all postpositions, which in your language would be prepositions, and I certainly would not presume to say which position is the better.

Anterior superior?
Posterior inferior?

Which position likest thee?
Either one is fine with me.

Anyway: "OF th'p'ple, BY th'p'ple, FOR th'p'ple." That, *mutatis mutandis*, is the effect. It is the style of the young radical progressives. In Tokyo you hear it almost any evening beside the statue of The Faithful Dog Hachiko in Puckery Gulch. I do not know where you hear it in Kyoto. In the governor's private chambers, perhaps.

Curious (all too curious), the police ear approached nearer. The wellwishers' platform was the setting for the incantation. Police inquiries were met, as was most proper, with silence, but a large banner identified the bund. Now the police would be hard put to prove in a court of law, and we do in spite of everything still have courts of law, that the young banner persons had not, all innocent of guile, found their banner in the streets. It is nonetheless my sober judgment that they were, in fact, boys of the bund. "Where do correct ideas come from? Do they drop from the skies? No." Is this not true, and does it not urge the conclusion I have reluctantly arrived at?

Whom were they seeing off, then? At whom were they incanting? These are the questions. The police have established that there were illegal departures that evening, doubtless with forged documents. It was the time of evening when the terminal is a can of worms, and planes seem to be shoving one another off the runways as *Zosterops japonica* off a branch. Yet the police think the most likely destination one of the American west-coast cities.

Initial destination, that is to say; and so you should be prepared. "Being prepared, we shall be able to deal properly with all kinds of complicated situations." The police do not seem concerned enough to have taken the matter up with the International Police Agency. It may be, indeed, that they think it an instance of good riddance.

Should you see my sister, tell her to write. At Craft her letters will be safe from unwanted scrutiny.

I cannot help thinking that there is a bond between you from a former life. It brought you together by a river in Kyoto, and now, perchance, it will bring you together on the wild frontier of America.

I do hope that you are taking care of yourself. How strange to think that for you, if I am using my conversion table properly, it is this morning. Amid the howling coyotes and the freely blowing winds, are there also joyous people's demonstrations?

40. Miss Shiraito to Mr. Brown

The end of Golden Week has come. Gentle mists hang over the Plain of Miyagi, and in them is a soft touch, that of spring. Elegant a maiden does feel, in an old garden, while frogs jump indefatigably in, and off in distant shrubbery an old woman gathers herbs for supper.

> Far from the madding rabble and its hubbubs
> Far from the teeming city and its suburbs,
> A granny plucks (beneath a twisted shrub) herbs
> Which soon she will convert into her sup herbs.

Today my brother and I must join the crowds pressing upon Tokyo from all sides. Am I sorry or glad to be leaving? I am sorry, I am glad. My grandmother's rustic stolidity (and also her Sendai accent) is a curative acting upon citytorn nerves and advanced awarenesses; and yet I cannot say that we accomplished one tiny thing, save perhaps to keep her away from Tokyo for a time. We transmitted my mother's invitation in exactly the ceremonious terms in which we received it.

All else is dominated by the fact that my grandmother and my father are in open alliance.

"And what shall we talk about tonight?" says my brother each evening after dinner, as the teakettle sings in the hearth.

"There has been no real answer to my very first question," said my grandmother yesterday evening.

"How funny you are! You make me want to laugh!" And I did, at some length.

"Life," continued my grandmother, as if philosophically, "is like crossing a pond on stepping stones. When you miss any of them none of the rest is as it should be. You are like any other little boy who thinks that the modern way is to walk on water. Suppose you have a time in the army."

"The Ground Self-Defense Force," said I. "It is unconstitutional by any name."

"The draft used to see all sorts of little lads through their difficult time. Only one of my sons, the least of them, actually waited for them to draft him, and then they didn't."

"The least of your sons? Please inform us who that was."

I must tell you one day soon about the pillow word, so important in our great lyrical tradition. For my grandmother "least of my sons" is a sort of pillow word, or phrase, going with my father. I think he likes it.

"He is improving, however. When he starts doing for little lads what they will not do for themselves, why then it may be that he is finally growing up."

"It all happened *years* ago," said I, seeking to dissemble. "The little lad in question lives out in the garden with her and the baby."

"I applauded when he started bringing his stray children home. It was among the very first things I found to applaud. When he sent one of them up here for me to dispose of, I was not so sure after all. And now I am beginning to be again, a little. When may I expect the happy news I probed for in my first question?"

You see how it was. My grandmother talked to my brother, and I talked to my grandmother, and my brother talked to no one at all.

He has been every day to visit my Sendai sister, actually my half-sister, to whom oblique reference is made in these last remarks. I have seen her only once. She came here on Friday looking very – well, you know how some women look as if they had always been pregnant. She has melted into Sendai, and

111

dresses as we did in Tokyo last week.

"How *funny* you are'"

"You could go on playing pinball in the army. It is my impression, from what I see about town, that pinball is the chief concern of the modern soldier, and sailor as well. Let us hope that if the Russians invade they are not clever enough to surround the pinball parlors."

"The Maritime Self-Defense Force is also unconstitutional. Might you have a copy of the constitution in the house?"

"I will hate to leave this garden," said my brother at length. "There is something about it."

"Why don't you come to Sendai? Sendai girls are strong."

"And so amusing. Laugh!" It was I, certain that she was not listening, but this time she did seem to be.

"Very well, laugh. But Sendai girls have something in their veins besides dietetic sugar water."

"That is as it is in each heart."

"What is in the veins usually gets there too."

"Ho hum," said my brother, with gestures.

"Ho hum," said my grandmother, taking up her night jar.

It is Children's Day, but the carp streamers which swell grandly in the spring winds tell us that boy children are the ones chiefly honored.

A mood descends over the land, I do not know whether of relief or of regret, when Golden Week is over. We still have the aftermath to be got through, and it may be a while before anything much is happening at House of Craft again. Patience must be the thing. *Dum spiro spero.*

41. Miss Shiraito to Mr. Brown

The warm east wind riffles the pendant racemes of wistaria. The trees over which the wistaria rambles darken with the summer. They are like brooding genii, and can have an effect upon the spirits. But never mind. "The darkness will pass." It will pass, I say, even as the moon passes through its time of darkness.

> Oh th'lunar thing will not much longer wane
> So too 'twill be (I think) with th' thing mundane.

How glad I was to find you home! I walked and walked, as my feet led me, and, looking up, found myself beneath your window! Lucky for me it was, as well, that I had chanced to bring my noodleman's tootler, and could render capably the little noodleman's tune. Lucky that you like noodles, and heard, and were hungry.

Two days have passed since my return from Sendai, and you made no mention of my Sendai letters. Under your desk blotter were two envelopes that looked astonishingly like the envelopes which I have been using since the beginning of the month, covered all over with azaleas, into which the inscription disappears ineffably.

You suddenly broke the meditative silence. You must get off a cable to Los Angeles, you said, about the visit of the Korean prime minister. I do admire the professional dedication of the persons who were up in Los Angeles at five in the morning to receive it.

I said, you will remember, that I would just wait for you to get the cablegram off.

You perhaps do not remember your reply. "That would be too kind of you." And you held the door open for me. "It will be late when I return, and I would worry about you, out alone in the darkness of this moonless night."

"God is my co-pilot."

It was on my mind to tell you about Mr. Rooby. I am sorry now that the meditative silence was so prolonged. One forgets, sometimes, that the claims of meditative silence are not absolute.

As I was walking past Kyobashi, which means Capital Bridge,

> What a Capital Bridge you are,

113

You are,
You are,
What a Capital Bridge you are,

I heard this voice singing. I turned to look. Few people even notice that it is a bridge any more, the waters beneath having been filled in to help the automobile on its way. There was Mr. Rooby, walking his Chihuahua, and looking very majestic, his beard trailing upon the warm spring breeze like clouds of glory.

"What a cute little tootler," said he, with American openness, not initially recognizing that it was I. "Let me have a tootle."

"It is a noodle tootler."

"That's very poetic."

He tootled, but not with distinction. He sounded like a masseuse all out of breath.

"Ho, it is you. I had not noticed, behind the tootler. And where are you tootling off to, purposefully in the night?"

"Wherever my fate may lead me." I meant "feet," but did not seek to correct the error. There was something very Japanese about it, I thought, in a contretemps with a foreigner. "What is your little Chihuahua's name?"

"Yoko."

"I thought it was a he Chihuahua."

"My dear! I bought her especially that I might name her Yoko. I have been wanting to tell you that I have not violated my probation. Not that the temptation has not been strong."

"To commit perjury again?"

"*Again*? No, to do something far worse. To rob the robbers right back. I cannot tell you how strong the temptation is each time I step inside a bank. Do you think your Craft lawyers might be able to help me with a plea of self-defense?"

"You told me you had held yourself short of having a bank account."

"That is just the point. I have to exchange dollars each time I need money, and so get robbed."

"*Piangi, o misero, piangi!*"

114

"But old Harry Gold says it is better not to have a bank account even if you do get robbed. Banks keep records and report things. He gets his in Honolulu, where no one can write."

Is this true? Does your newspaper have an office in Honolulu?

"I can ask our lawyers, if you wish, though perhaps you might acquaint me better with the facts."

"The facts about old Harry should interest you more. You and that creepy newspaper friend of yours." Now I wonder how he knows about you? "Harry says it was a mistake not to do everything, everything, in Honolulu. He is getting nervous. If that creepy newspaper friend of yours wants his scoop he had better hurry. I see you are in a hurry yourself. Well, good-bye, if it must be."

"Good-bye. Good-bye, Yoko." I reached down to pat her head, which was not easy to find among the teeth, and let my feet lead me yet farther northwards.

Mr. Rooby and Yoko had apparently walked as far as they meant to walk. The former put the latter into a doggy bag, and with a "He *is* a creep" on the part of the former, they entered the Upper Ginza subway station.

Summer came in yesterday, at just one moment past noon. Now begin the days of waiting for the first cuckoo. It has been a thing, in our great lyrical tradition, to urge, just at this time of the year, that cuckoos show a little more initiative.

> Pray sing now in May,
> *Cuculus canorus.*
> Will'st thou wait and bore us
> In the June-time chorus
> Of all of the *Cuculidae?*

There – thirty-one famous Japanese syllables, by one beloved of an emperor long ago, translated into thirty-one English, and with rhymes, too. It is what you call a tour, I believe, de force.

I thought you looked a bit peaked, but maybe it was only the contrast with the badger.

And did the people of Los Angeles start up from their beds upon receipt of your cablegram?

42. Mr. Brown to Miss Gray

The wistaria is in bloom. It is my favorite flower. Trailing its lavender sprays upon the early-summer breeze, a wistaria cannot be other than elegant. On a walk up north of the park the other day, I came upon a person hacking down a lovely, lovely wistaria in full bloom. Why, said I. Why? Because his automobile required a place to park, said he. This made sense. The automobile, a Subaru, which means Pleiades, which is a part of Taurus, which makes it a little bull of an automobile, was then parked on the sidewalk. Japan is a crowded country. Automobiles have a hard time of it.

Also in bloom is the azalea, most ill-mannered of flowers. I think of it as the noisy magpie of the floral world. Or the black-leather crowd, maybe.

> Here wistaria, shy, as if frightened.
> There azalea, pushy and strident.

Which will do for the moment.

Two of my telephones have been ringing energetically, in permutations and combinations. The man who installed the third telephone, just the other day, said he was a bachelor too, and quite understood.

"It is necessary that one be able to tell them apart. Yours sound far too similar to one another. Let me, if I may without offense, recommend to you –" and it was like choosing a cast for your opera.

The third one is unlisted. I had not thought to have an unlisted telephone, because no one in this country ever uses the directory. It is full of Suzukis, so what is the point? I had not, however, thought of the readiness with which people trouble

116

the information operators. So now I have this unlisted number.

"Two telephones busy all the time," said Miss S. "You must have a great deal of company."

"How do you know, if you do not call?"

"One does."

In the land where intuitions grow.

I have become almost neurotic about defending myself against these encroachments. One does.

> Now that thou hast safely flown,
>> I needs must tell thee that the telly
> (Vision too, but more so) phone
>> Hath made of me a nervous Nelly.

I think it must be an instinct that my family (Braun, it used to be) picked up in the Thirty Years War: let no one approach the castle; have encounters at a distance from it.

Night before last I saw her come purposefully up the street, and then she started blowing on a silly little horn. I could not resist opening a window and calling down for a bowl of noodles.

She came up, and there followed mostly silence. There usually does.

"I am bored," said I, after a time of it.

The change from passivity to tragic reproach was like one of those quick changes on the Kabuki stage.

"Oh, I do not mean by any means that I am bored at this moment with this company. You do not think, surely, do you, that if that were the case I would have spoken of it? No. I mean that Tokyo is an unsatisfying place to report from. Little is recognized as news. I sometimes think of asking for a transfer to Hong Kong. A reporter from Hong Kong will be guaranteed a by-line as long as that giant goes on dying. It promises to be a long time."

She shifted the large, weighty bag in which she keeps dictionaries and, I am sure, a tape recorder.

"Oh, I do hope not."

"But I thought you wanted him to go on dying forever."

"I mean, I hope you will not ask for a transfer. I would miss

117

you. I cannot tell you how much."

"I doubt that I will, really. We must arrange for a story from Tokyo to make editors vomit. We are doing well so far."

In silence, she turned to pruning and fertilizing. She talks a great deal when we are in the library of House of Craft, or the Press Club, or the squish and gabble of Foojy House; but here it seems her purpose to occupy in silence. Sometimes she prunes and fertilizes, and sometimes she does not.

"Just try asking in Japanese at a jewelry store for a ruby or a diamond or a sapphire –"

"I've never done it."

"– just try asking in Japanese, and you'll get English back, or maybe a question mark. Isn't that interesting?"

It is all she said on what may be called the subject. Finally I said that I had to go out.

I find it hard to judge whether the appearance of not knowing is real or feigned. Such remarks as this make me think that for the most part it is feigned. I hope so. She is more amusing that way, and I need not reprove myself so sternly for using her as I do, and not employing her brother.

I suppose that before long spring will have come even to the windswept plains whereon you dwell. Do you know what a pillow word, or phrase, is?

> Of the seeds of Iris sedosas
> Which grow in episcopal closes
> (I doubt it, but I'm in
> Dire need of enrhyming),
> The plumage of brachyrinchoses.

There. A massive pillow phrase. And why do I speak of such, and introduce an example? Because your description of your plains has come to make "windswept" seem like a pillow word.

You have reaccultured yourself as I would have expected, in a sound and sensible manner. I have no doubt that by the time the pasqueflowers bloom you will feel as much at home as we birds of passage ever do. I was very glad to hear from you, and will be next time too.

43. Miss Shiraito to Miss Gray

In the breezes there are already the feel and the scent of early summer. It is neither cold nor warm. The last petals of wistaria are upon the pond a lavender veil, and upon the dark earth, peony-colored, lie great petals of peony. Meanwhile azaleas fill all the unoccupied corners of spring with their several shades of magenta and cerise.

And how is it with you? Does the Indian love song ring out over the plains?

Are you well?

It is of my fugitive sister that I must write to you. Mr. Brown has indicated a reluctance to talk of her, and of my brother as well.

The Concerned White Lilies are these days off at the American embassy demonstrating in behalf of Arabs, and so there are no barricades which I can approach. I do, however, have a fico or two which I may venture to pass on to you. Yesterday morning there was an exchange between my mother and father.

"Have you revised your views as to whether and when she will be back?"

"As to whether, no. As to when, yes. How nice of that spider to bring you within easy earshot."

I was gathering things for the mynah bird, and had drawn near, and so was able to hear over the screeching of the azaleas, as Mr. Brown would say. (He is very amusing on the subject.)

"In which direction have you revised it?"

"The less expensive one."

There the matter ended. My mother was right to ask no more. We all of us know when wit is about to raise its head.

There is one more small thing.

Passing the post office on our way to the station yesterday evening, several of us girls had our palms read. There are those who say that when you have had your palm read once you have had it read for all time, but I do not agree. We have so little to go on.

119

"There is this line, you will observe," said my palmistress, "veering thus before taking off. Observe its detachment, so unlike the helter-skelter (you must forgive the expression) of the rest of your palm. Observe, if you will, where it seems to be leading, into the wild blue yonder."

A shudder of recognition passed over me.

"The wild blue yonder" – it is not possible to think, is it not, that there is not a bond between you from former lives? There was your coming upon her in Kyoto, and now there is – I scarcely know what. A shudder passes over me again of nameless recognition. Call me occult, if you will.

It is a time of *tristesse*, this time when spring gives way to summer. Petals lie upon the earth and upon the waters, and into the breeze there comes the somehow rancid scent of summer; and we know that even as there is fruition there is over-ripeness and decay.

> When summer says to spring: "Away! Away!"
> It is in vain to make reply: "Stay! Stay!"
> The summer grasses round my hut grow dense,
> And nightingales (like Arabs) fold their tents.

44. Miss Shiraito to Mr. Brown

Green, green, and green wherever one looks; and bit by bit summer seems to gather substance. I wish we had not done away with summertime. The presence of it on the far shore of the ocean adds an hour to the time difference, and makes Professor Gray, on and beyond that shore, seem yet farther away.

It is good that you are susceptible to the sounds of the Tokyo night, and that my little ruse brought you again to a window. I almost think I should, at this point, discourage you from further study of our culture. You have come just the right distance. If you knew all about it, why then you would recognize the amateurishness of such performances as mine.

I am glad, I say, to have seen you, and your *Citrus tachibana*, and the rest. Yet I came away feeling rebuffed.

You say that you did not receive my Sendai letters. In this I suspect that you do not speak the truth.

How came you, last night, to ask, quite out of the blue: "Been getting any good pillow words lately?" How came you to do so if you did not receive the second of my Sendai letters? And if you received the second and not the first, it would have impelled you to make inquiry about the latter.

"I know a police inspector in Honolulu, and nowhere in the world is there a lovelier place for moonlighting," you said.

And I thought: would that we might, one day or night, do it together, Mr. Brown and I.

There was pleasure in the thought. Yet the unstated answer to the question about my brother rings through the quiet of this night of gibbous moonlight. Very well; something else must be made to come to mind. I cannot just at the moment think what it will be. I wish I might soon owe Professor Gray a letter.

Without further adieux, I leave you.

That came of its own accord, and seems determined to stay. So it is that the lyrical impulse wells up, despite strong feelings that the time is not right.

> When one thinks one will eschew
> Without additional adieux
>   These things pivotal,
> Enters of its own accord
> A paronomastic word,
>   Next to total-
>   Ly pivotal.

I think of you, silver, in the light of this moon; and I am at once less sad and more pensive.

45. Mr. Brown to Miss Gray

On your side of the world you enter Gemini. On our side we enter, my almanac tells me, the Fortnight of Small Satisfaction.

So busy a time, as they say in this place, that one wants to borrow the services of the cat. The mad bombers, they who for the past months have been righting the wrongs of the world by planting bombs in buildings similar to Miss Shiraito's, which however escaped, have been apprehended. Miss Shiraito's sister might well have been among them, but was not. Letters to the editor of the *Morning Flush* tell us what nice young people they are, essentially and inwardly. There is probably truth in it, and we need not have been surprised had a pretty White Lily been among them. But none was.

Fortunately the weather has been cool. At this time of the year a wave of muggy air will push up from Okinawa, only to be pushed back again by a wave of cold air from the Sea of Okhotsk. Though suspicious by nature of things from the Sea of Okhotsk, I must say that in this case I find it the more sympathetic of the two.

> How pleasant it must be
> Up there on the Okhotsk Sea,
> Where the crabs and the codfishes play,
> And the skies are not cloudy all day.

The above is by way of apology for my neglect. Thus do we remind people that they owe us letters. I am aware, of course, that it is a time of academic festivals, and doubtless you too have been busy. But I like to apologize. I have been here long enough that I have acquired the habit.

There arrived this morning by special delivery a flaming red letter from Miss Shiraito, embossed all over with yet more flaming peonies. One can often tell from the color of a letter what its contents are going to be. I once had a series of summonses from the tax office, on papers of increasingly insistent hue; and when we reached the reds of high saturation and medium brilliance which you see on May Day, I thought it best to go around and see what they wished of me. The contents of Miss Shiraito's letter are restrained, but the envelope tells me that her resentment is great at my having declined to give employment to the pinball brother. So be it.

I am sorry that I cannot help her in this matter, because she is a good friend, really, and because she has been such a help to me. It was she, of course, who got me started on the Craft thing, and it, more than the thing of the mad bombers, keeps me busy. I have a sense of urgency. So many little bits of information tell me that if the story is to be mine I must make haste.

Let me give you an instance.

This afternoon her Mr. Gold and a bearded person who can only have been her Mr. Rooby were having bloody Marys (Bloody Maries?) and bar dice in the Press Club. They both know who I am, but they did not lower their voices one bit. The latter probably does not care and the former does not know that I am on the story.

"Been getting much lately?" asked Mr. Rooby, a round of dice having ended.

"Oh, about the same. And you?"

"You have misunderstood me. I meant for your peanuts. I have none."

"You must think I have just about the filthiest mind. I can't be sure, really, you know, to answer your interesting question. It is like being a quarterback and not knowing which side people are on."

"'In this world things are complicated, and decided by many factors.'"

"More so by far in this hemisphere than in the other. If I don't know whose side people are on, I do know, or think I know, that they will find ways not to answer questions, and answer questions about questions about questions, etc. It is not so on the other. When the questions start coming, they will all be like frightened children."

This accords with things I have had from Miss S. and others; and so I work hard.

I like Mr. Rooby and Mr. Gold. One can, you know, even New York types. So things are interesting, here in the Fortnight of Small Satisfaction. I hope they are not too dull over there in Gemini. Miss S. says that she is sorry she does not owe you a letter. Because I have been such a disappointment, she wants to talk to you about the brother. What tidings of the sister?

46. Miss Gray to Miss Shiraito

It is spring, such spring as we have in this strange, sad climate.

One cannot be sure that winter is past until summer has come. My father says that he has seen snow, here on the plains and not in the mountains, every month of the year, and I have seen it myself every month except July. We had pasqueflowers and wild plums earlier in the month, and now the lilacs are coming into bloom, solatium for the lack of wistaria.

So it may be said that we are having spring, and now too we are having evening. In the evening the wind that has all day long been blowing in over the plains ceases to do so, and a liquid calm settles over the land, so that not even the leaves of the cottonwoods and aspens stir. In an hour it will start up again and blow all through the night. This is the good hour, which I would like you to see and feel some time.

Thank you for the interesting report on your sister. As in the Kyoto days, I keep thinking I see her. It is the time of the year when the street people are most numerous. They advance with the line of the spring, and move on to the mountains.

Some afternoons ago, beside the creek behind the auditorium, I tried something.

"Miss Shiraito, I presume?" said I, to a person.

"Yankee go home," came the response.

It was an illustration of an interesting truth, that you Japanese never leave home. You take home with you.

The next time I crossed the creek behind the auditorium, I

found the same encampment, or one so similar as to be indistinguishable from it.

"Miss Shiraito, I presume?" said I once more, this time to no person in particular.

My question was this time received in silence. Now silence is a wondrous thing. There are all kinds of it, conveying all manner of meanings. We are told, and with truth, that it can say more than words.

> More eloquent than those of logorrhea
> The changes to be rung on aphonia.

This silence had a studied quality about it.

Today I again took a little stroll down there, but the encampment had folded its tents. It has probably moved on to the mountains.

If indeed my query meant something, then did it relate to your sister, or to someone else by the same name? I remember your telling me that your surname has exactly the same incidence in the Tokyo telephone directory as Seidensticker, and so the latter possibility seems slim.

Please remember me to your family. I think fondly of them.

47. Miss Gray to Mr. Brown

People like to say of these high landlocked regions that spring lasts a weekend. This must be the weekend. The day is warm and sunny and lilacs are in effusive bloom. I went for a long walk through the pastures this afternoon, keeping a sharp eye out for burrs and rattlesnakes, far more in evidence than deer and antelope, far, far more than crabs and codfishes. It is among the wonders of this culture that there are no paths for walking. That is not quite true. There are trails in the mountains, but on the plains there are no evidences that anyone until I came along ever took a walk. Everything, indeed, discourages

125

walking. I sometimes wonder if ranchers might not have planted burrs and encouraged rattlesnakes, as an English squire would plant gorse and encourage foxes.

> Oh the squire has his foxes and his furze,
> And the rancher has his rattlesnakes and burrs.

Your columbines are beginning to come out, and there are little clumps of iris in the wind. It seems to be the only imported flower that can hold out unassisted against our hard, dry summers. You see them in the pioneer cemeteries, bits of Kew, to tell you how little the pioneers liked the land they had come to.

If you find Miss Shiraito silently pruning and fertilizing and otherwise seeking to run your life, I find her influencing mine by remote control – by *remoko*, as they say over there. I see a Shiraito behind every bush.

There have been little gifts. Little things have come in envelopes bearing near-by postmarks. Still lifes have been left at my door. One evening there will be a geranium, another a petunia. They suggest the propensities of a certain family.

There have been telephone calls. There were several which I sought to encourage, as we Americans will, with a cheery hello, and which went no further. Then, upon a hunch, I late one evening replaced hello with *moshimoshi*.

There was a tiny gasp, a she-gasp, I judged it to be, and the person whom I sought to engage in conversation hung up.

Then yesterday evening, to my *moshimoshi*, there came an answer.

"Forgive me for summoning you to the telephone. Though we have not been introduced, I hope you are well. I bring to you the greetings of Miss Yoko Shiraito."

These remarks were as if written out and memorized, and delivered in uncertainty that they would make it.

"How very nice," said I. "And to whom have I the honor of speaking?"

There was a pause, pregnant with incomprehension.

Then: "Excuse me?"

"I asked who you might be."

"A friend."

"You must come and introduce yourself."

"I am in Memphis."

"And will you be coming nearer?"

"For the nonce."

On this philological note our conversation ended.

I told the operator that I had had an objectionable call, and asked to have it traced. It had come from a pay telephone down on Broadway. I thought of rushing down, but it was late and I was tired.

More and more we have street people. They move on and become mountain people, montagnards. In the fall they will come throuqh again, and then, when the frost is on the pumpkin (actually we have no pumpkins), they will move on to more clement regions. It is an ill wind, Mr. Brown, from which the cooper does not profit.

I await further tidings of your jolly bagman and your scoop. Sing ho the jolly bagman and the scoop!

48. Miss Shiraito to Mr. Brown

Summer is coming, and already there are intimations of the long, gloomy rains, when a maiden sits at home, and waits, for she knows not what. Here under my eaves the flower is the Chinese pink (*Dianthus chinensis*). One thinks of the pink as a shrinking flower, but if any pink shrinks it is the Japanese (*Dianthus superbus*) and not the Chinese.

We also have hydrangeas, here in this garden in the western marches, and iris, and in among the darkling plantings at a greater distance there are huge flowers of that greatest of magnolias, *Magnolia grandiflora*. Orange blossoms there are too, *Citrus tachibana*, for us, and not rosemary, the thing that

brings remembrance. If yours is also coming into bloom, do you
also remember?

> On smelling the tachibana
> That blooms in genial May
> I find it smells as of the sleeve
> Of an old mate whom I did leave.

It is an old and famous poem Englished by an esteemed
translator. Save to inquire how the first rhyme was meant to
work, and to observe that the lunar fifth month is far more June
than May, I would not presume to comment upon it, or to
suggest revision.

And now come great swarms of cuckoos, making us feel silly
that a few weeks ago (cf. my last letter but one) we were
seeking impatiently to coax the early birds on.

> O cuckoo, now thou com'st to roost.
> To bring back mem'ries, thou cockoo'st;

It is Sunday. Out among the streets, less and less seems to
happen on Sundays, which used to be the liveliest of days.
Customs change. Here at home things do happen on Sundays,
when people tend to be present in larger numbers. This morning at breakfast there was a scene.

My father was the last to straggle in. I had been about to
straggle out myself.

"And how will the dear *Flush* set about ruining our breakfast
this morning?" said he, taking it unceremoniously from my
brother.

Upon seeing what has happened to the Giants, my brother
usually has no further shrift for the *Flush*. This season they are
losing more frequently than they are winning, and so the shrift
tends to be very short indeed.

This morning it was different. "I had not finished reading all I
wished to read in the *Flush*," he said, reaching to take it back
again.

"Congratulations," said my father, turning to the ham and
eggs which is (are?) his Sabbath breakfast. "I did not think that

you still knew how. This egg is overdone and the farther one is underdone. How did you manage anything so delicate?"

"Somewhere right along there where they run together should be exactly right," said my brother. "Eat that."

My mother started down into the garden.

My brother at length put down the *Flush*, which my father, however, did not take up.

"I have had thoughts of things," said the latter.

"Congratulations," said the former. "I did not think that you still knew how."

"Do you wish to be informed of the content of the thoughts? I thank you most feelingly for your congratulations. Perhaps you will wish to take them back when informed of the content."

"Is it that you have penetrated to the still heart of things?"

"I did that some time ago, and found it very still. Now I have returned to the surface."

"We may make a distinction, perhaps, between thoughts of superficial things and superficial thoughts of things. And then again, perhaps we may not."

"It is a good distinction. Let us make it, and let us marvel for a moment at your cleverness in having come upon it."

"Of what superficial things have your thoughts been?"

"Of you."

"Everything I am I owe to you."

I was startled. Whatever my brother may be, he is seldom indelicate.

"You acknowledge the debt, do you?" A compounding of the indelicacy! My mother looked in from the garden. Our eyes seemed to meet at the same spot upon the veranda.

"I do. I do indeed. I have measured it carefully, and mean to make repayment in kind, one of these times."

"May I understand you to say that you mean to show a little respect for that in the case of which you have just acknowledged indebtedness?"

"My measurements do not reveal anything which calls for respect."

"Let me tell you what my own survey of the dimensions of the

129

problem would seem to have revealed to me. I am informed by it that you will soon have complete and utter independence. I look upon this as a gamble which must be taken, and I hope that you have sufficient regard for yourself to do likewise. Well. Here is that Shiraito Yoko person again." He had at length taken up the *Morning Flush*. "She tells our editor that, in the matter of the Korean school, Governor Minobe is right and a long list of other people are wrong. She says that all persons are siblings, and we must dismiss from our minds, etc., artificial distinctions about nation and race. Some people will believe anything. If I were you I would be ashamed to go by the same name. I would indeed."

My brother stayed to the end of my father's breakfast, a sign, I fear, that he was in some disarray. The mynah bird was the chief beneficiary, because of the energy with which my mother gathered things.

In the matter of the *Citrus tachibana*, I have consulted *The Fruitiest and the Nuttiest*, the recognized authority, and think that my diagnosis was not wrong. The rampantly raging shoot which seems to fill you with apprehension and glee, and in the case of which you set me that amusing verbal problem –

> Upon the *tachibana* tree
> A sucker, swelling, grew
> Oh find, said he, oh find for me,
> A most ingenious simile.
> Well, what about bamboo? –

yes, it is without question a sucker. It must be cut. The *Citrus tachibana* must be suckered. (Oh! Oh! Oh! A next to perfect pivot word! And it came as if by inflatus!) (My proposed simile, offered in the last line above as a solution to the amusing problem, is flawed by the fact that it is out of season; but in an earlier season the many varieties of bamboo do all of them have that same rampantly raging quality.)

Will you lend my brother the money to go and stay with Professor Gray for a few weeks or months or so? She said that anyone in the family would be most welcome at any time, and I think that if my father and grandmother could be persuaded that he is in danger of taking up with a blue-eyed foreign lady, they might be persuaded, further, to accept his disinclination to take up with any lady at all.

Am I right in thinking that I write to you more often under the waning moon than at other times? What do you suppose this means? Sleep well, whatever.

49. Mr. Brown to Miss Shiraito

Not being a part of the wealthy establishment of your land, I have had to choose between a roof over my head and an air conditioner, or, as you people call it, a room cooler. I have chosen the former. There are they who have made the other choice. I see them, down in the park, or in their Cadillacs and Continentals, and if this genial sultriness persists I may go down and join them.

> Oh the rich gets richer and the poor gets poorer
> So its down to the park with my room cooler.

Of the things you have given me, several threaten to shoot straight through the roof. Thus there is the *Citrus tachibana*. I liked your poem, and I think in the matter of the sucker your advice, and that of your authority, must soon be taken. It puts me in mind of a famous haiku, eighteenth century, thought by some to be elegant, and by some, not.

> Upon, of the tachibana tree,
> The sucker, lies the dew.
> Although a most excellent simile,
> I'd not, myself, choose bamboo.

And then there is the *hechima* which you brought round. It has pendant objects all to the very top, and the top is getting farther away by the moment. Should I cut it, in the interests of saving the roof of my balcony and the floor of that of my upstairs neighbor (thought by some to be Korean)? Or would that have a discouraging effect upon the objects so vigorously lengthening and swelling?

> Snake gourd or sponge gourd,
> Cylindrical loofah.
> In "Brown's Distent Creepers,"
> *Daszmascha daroofa.*

I have not written in a very long while, and who knows when I will write again? It is like us Americans, this not knowing. I have therefore given you more than one outpouring of lyricism, in hopes of being on top of things.

As to the business at hand. In your recent letter the topic immediately before the waning moon is the one that requires attention. There is an expression which Kenkyusha renders "dig round the root of the tree." You botany majors of course know what it means, without the help you may expect from Kenkyusha: the preparation of roots for the shock of transplantation. Have you made the necessary preparations in the case of your brother? Has he agreed to the undertaking? Does he know what it means to live in Redrock, with or without a blue-eyed foreign lady? There are no pinball parlors. America is a poor country. And have you, by the bye, informed Miss Gray of your project?

I will think about it, and let you know. I will call you.

Today, as I fought my way in a southwesterly direction past the "scramble crossing" in front of Foojy House, I saw Mr. Gold and Mr. Rooby doing the same thing, in a northeasterly direction. I spun about and followed them into Foojy House, where I took a table on the opposite side of the hedge.

They had nice things to say about you.

"Do you think she has had plastic surgery?"

"The elevator girl?"

"No, no, *no*. Plastic surgeons go in for little shrinking noses, not big swooping ones."

"They go in for whatever they see in the commercials.

Barbra Streisand's is the big nose these days."

"Oh, I hope not. Just think of it, Barbra Streisands all up and down Ginza.

"But I meant our other friend, the tea pourer."

"I don't think so. She would have told me. She is a confider."

"They all are. Is she more so?"

"Well, I think she is sort of a mutual kind, kind of. I named my Chihuahua after her."

"And told her all about me. Did you tell her that I'm also a mutual type?"

So you see they like you.

After a time Mr. Gold laid down his spoon. The Super Goobers seemed to distend before his attack, like the mushrooms in the play, or a cylindrical loofah.

"You see more of her than I do, and I never see her alone. Does she tell you anything about the state of nerves, up there on the top floor? I do not expect them to crack. What the president really gets from his flower-arranging teacher is lessons in toughness. But it would help me to arrange my schedule if I knew about the general state."

"What does it matter? Assuming you are still as sure as you used to be that they will not answer questions about questions, etc."

"It is a barometer. The state of nerves is a delicate instrument giving us information about impulses far far away."

"I suppose what I understand least, among the impulses emerging from you yourself, is how you can be sure that your peanuts are getting where you want them to get."

"Oh, the men of Craft would long since have defalcated unless at least some of my peanuts made it. Had a quiet defalcation."

Now *there* is an interesting word for you.

I quoted you in my obituary for the former prime minister. Unable to get past the switchboard of House of Craft, I stopped by the *Flush* and asked to see the letters on the subject which were likely to make the "Outcry" page. They all said the same thing in very much the same words, and so I felt safe. The gentleman who showed me the letters was helpful. He remembered you and agreed that I was in no danger of misquoting you. I need not apologize, I am sure, though it will give me much pleasure to do so if you wish.

I have been meaning to reprove you, gently, for charging me with the introduction of corrupt diphthongs into your name. Would anyone guilty of that offense have called you sésquipedálian Míss Shiraíto?

50. Miss Shiraito to Miss Gray

It is May Day by the old calendar. I suppose it would be futile of me to recommend to the people that they have their May Day by the old calendar. May Day is, by the old calendar, always a lucky day. By the new, the people must take their chances. This year, yes, it was lucky, and my files inform me that I took advantage of this fortuitous coincidence to write cheerfully to both you and Mr. Brown from Sendai. Most years, no.

But of course the fact must also be considered that we enter the time of the gloomy rains, the plum rains. It rains and it does not rain. One cannot be without an umbrella, and yet one finds all too often that an umbrella is no protection from fine mists of rain that seem to fold in from all sides. And suddenly, in all the groves, where the plums come into fruition, and that is why they are called plum rains, it is summer.

> Suddenly, suddenly, all now is summery,
> In the orangerie and in the plummerie.

I certainly was very interested in your musings and surmisings about my sister. I have not shared them with the rest of my family. My father's jocularity is so impenetrable, and besides, it would only be a matter of time before they were in the hands of that assistant chief of police who was a kindergarden inmate along with him.

Bits of information do also come the other way, not through my father but through my mother, though it has to be that she gets them from him, when they are together.

The police can find out most things they want to find out, and when they do not you can be fairly sure that they do not.

"It is because of your father that they took the trouble," said my mother, pouncing on a dor, than which the mynah bird loves nothing more. "We should all be very grateful."

> Said my mother, pouncing on a dor,
> Than which the mynah bird loves nothing more.

It gives you a feeling, when these things come of their own accord, that poetry is not made by man alone.

"Pshaw, Mother," said I. "Pshaw."

"Why?"

"Pshaw, that's all."

"They would not have taken the trouble except for your father. I know it. Only a mother can know these things."

What had happened is that the police had gone to very considerable trouble (or some computer had – the police can afford computers even if none of the rest of us can). Checking passport applications against exit cards, they had come to the conclusion that on the night of the airport incident several members of the bund took a non-stop flight for Los Angeles.

"Pshaw, is what I say."

"And *I* say that they would not have thought it necessary except for your father. What do they care if a few spongers go and sponge off a foreign country for a time? (That is what your father says.)"

"What do they care if the talents of a few sincere young people are wasted at the corners of the earth?"

"Your father says he keeps wishing the Koreans would take it more easily in the matter of young spongers, but they will not listen to his advice."

"Chairman Mao knows what to do with sincere young people."

"Doesn't he just, though. (I am quoting your father once

135

more. My own opinion is of no interest to anyone.)"

There were scattered instances that night of people departing fraudulently in all directions, but the most considerable group departed for Los Angeles. Two or three seem to have gone to Korea, which certainly is very curious, unless they had in mind contradictions.

And so if my sister is indeed in that arroyo in Redrock, you can introduce yourself, and have a nice, long visit. It may be that when she returns she will get the book thrown at her, as they say, for violating the passport and egress regulations. The police have strange ways of welcoming people home. But do not tell her so, and have a nice, long visit.

In the affairs of my younger older brother, I have made another modest proposal to Mr. Brown. He seems to think it important that I inform you of it, even though he is aware of my wish not to trouble you with those affairs. The heart of the proposal is that my younger older brother be persuaded to emulate the bold example of my sister. It is beyond me to know why you should be troubled, at this early stage.

I certainly was very glad to hear about the lilacs. Here the lilac tends to be a wan, bedraggled thing. It is curious that Russian things seem to do less well here than Chinese things. The fact is among those upon which my father does not tire of remarking.

51. Miss Shiraito to Mr. Brown

The rain clouds of June blot out the new moon, the tendrils of the morning glory lengthen. Lotus leaves emerge upon the surface. At the brink of the pond where they do so, hydrangeas are in bloom. Soon all the marks of summer will be ranged side by side, and the air of summer will be heavy upon them. I can feel it already, indeed.

I know not why it is I am so gloomy. It is as if, with dark

verdure imposed upon a dark sky, a darkness of the spirit chose to add another facet.

> an iris floating upon waters deep
> although not knowing why it is I weep

The poetry of our great lyrical tradition was not punctuated, nor, indeed, was much of anything else. I give you the above instance to show you what clever people they were, to understand all the same. And how very great, without punctuation, you will observe, is the increment of ambiguity. It is curious that none of those gifted translators seem to have thought of the device. The poem, the two hundred twenty-third in the eighth of our court anthologies, was sent to the greatest of our lady romancers by the lady next door. This information I provide for your divertissement and sentimental education. It makes a person feel better, on a heavy-spirited morning, to have done some good.

In the matter of the former late prime minister, I fear I think you fibbed. Few people here read the *Los Angeles Times*, and little harm was done; but no letter which the *Flush* would have considered printing would have had so little hostility in it.

Yesterday there was a meeting in Mr. Kuromaku's office, attended by Mr. Minawata, Mr. Gold, and him. Mindful of your interest, and of the unwritten request in your most recent letter, I listened carefully and made careful notes. I think I am able to steep and pour tea at a more leisurely pace than most persons because my father was in Tokyo University with Mr. Kuromaku.

My first cup was of Japanese green tea. Pleasantries were being exchanged.

"We are proud of our view," said Mr. Kuromaku. "That is the palace, and those are its little buildings, and big buildings, and there are its moat and circumferential wall."

"I recognized them," said Mr. Gold.

"Sometimes in the winter," said Mr. Minawata, doing his part, "we can see Mt. Fuji."

"How do you spell it?" said Mr. Gold.

"Have you seen Mt. Fuji?" said Mr. Kuromaku, ignoring the question if he understood it, which I rather doubt. When Mr. Gold says, as he does, that they speak better English than he, it is nice, but I think he means to flatter.

"And there is the police building," said he, "that ugly, ugly tower. See how near it suddenly seems."

On my second cup of tea, which we call red and you call black, and I sometimes muse on what the difference tells us, the mood seemed congratulatory.

"So that," said Mr. Kuromaku, sagely, bringing his hands together, and using all ten fingers, in the way recommended by Chairman Mao for playing the piano, "is that."

"It has not been easy," said Mr. Minawata, only, as becomes a subordinate, less sagely, "but I think we have done well."

"Thank you, Miss Shiraito, for this tea, which you call red and we call black." The weird way he sometimes has of seeming to read a person's thoughts! "The symbolism would be better if it were the reverse. Your balance gets blacker and blacker, and ours, meanwhile, redder and redder."

"Let us not think of that. Let us think rather of the redness of this day as it is lettered upon the calendar."

"I do not doubt that our relations will get better and better."

> Oh a red-letter day
> Is a get-better day,

I hummed to myself, to the tune of "Turkey in the Straw." I had the beginning of a poem, awaiting an occasion. (Do you think I might be called an occasional poetess?)

"Don't mention it," I paused to say, as I backed out the door. For the third round I brought coffee.

An air of anxiety seemed to have replaced that of felicitation.

"'We have so much to learn from the Americans.' I quote the former prime minister, not the late one, the other, once more. It is something I am always saying to the people in our Los Angeles office. 'There are times,' I am always saying to them. It is not us of Craft I am worried about, you will of course understand, but all of the poor hardworking little travel agents

138

who will suffer if something goes wrong with the Waikiki thing. (Mrs. Kuromaku sends her regards.)"

"What do your Los Angeles people say, when you tell them that there are times?"

"Oh, you are the one who must inform us. We have so much to learn."

"Well, I would enlarge upon your interesting statement by saying that there are times when I am glad I am not a Japanese."

Mr. Kuromaku and Mr. Minawata looked at him as if this were the most incomprehensible of several such statements.

"I know where I am going if it all starts oozing out, but I cannot think where you are going, poor dear fellows. Just see how that ugly ugly tower seems to come near us in the play of light and shadow."

Mr. Kuromaku, whose back was to the window, as the back of a chairman always is, turned to look.

"And what do you mean by 'if,' etc.," said Mr. Minawata, his ten fingers once more together. They were twitching slightly, as if in happy dreams.

"I have never seen a country so full of them."

"Of what?"

"Of etces."

He looked up at me, and I felt that I had to leave, before Mr. Kuromaku turned back from his survey of the police building, lest I flush.

He (Mr. Gold) asked me to marry him before he left, but that is neither here nor there.

My mother and Dr. Madder say that there is very little you can do about the bugs on the *Prunus mume* but pick them off one by one and crush them between your fingernails.

I hope your failure to put in an appearance at the Press Club these six and ninety hours does not mean that the unsettled state of the skies has had an unsettling effect upon your spirits. You must tell yourself that every cloud has a silver lining.

52. Mr. Brown to Miss Gray

Happy Friday the Thirteenth!

When one system of truths collides with another, which do you choose? That is the question. A person's deeper loyalties must at such times show themselves. Let mine show themselves as I say it to you again: Happy Friday the Thirteenth!

Miss S. is right when she says that in fullness one smells decay. Down upon the lake the lotus leaves send forth a most wonderful scent, a most deliciously spicy one, and I do not know why it makes me think of funerals, unless I have been here too long, and everything about this ramshackle city has begun to take on the look of autumn leaves before the wind. I sometimes stop and marvel that nothing I see around me is more than a quarter of a century old. Do I like it? Do I not like it? Yes and no.

You will have heard from her. I told her she must tell you of her plans for you, and she is obedient in these matters. Does the prospect fill you with delight, of running an underground railroad for the clan Shiraito? The brother's problem is a classical one, the problem, indeed, of the Shining Genji. He yearns for Mother. Of this you should be warned.

> The cuckoo bird, or so I gather,
> Yearns for Mother, not for Father.

I have been very busy, in pursuit of the story I am after. Let me tell you of the most recent helper I have come upon. He promises to be most helpful.

Yesterday I passed Mr. Rooby, him of that amusing affair down in Kyoto. He was scrambling northeastwards across the Foojy House intersection, as if all googaw for Foojy House goo. Turning, I followed him inside, and bought a ticket for a Yam Jamboree.

I sat shouting at waitresses who were indifferent to my needs and looking around to see what all the others were having. You can do it, you know, when you have paid your money and are hungry.

The things people were having looked vaguely bicentennial. Mr. Rooby seemed, like me, to prefer the rich browns of the Yam Jamboree. I did finally stop a waitress, and then I let my eye seem to fall accidentally on him.

"Hello there."

"Hello there."

"How's the Yam Jamboree?"

"The worst yet."

"The worst Yam Jamboree yet?"

"The worst anything yet."

"You should have told me."

"'*Chacun*, Mr. Brown, *a son goût*,' I thought, as I saw the ticket you were waving around."

"I know you too. I see you at the Press Club, and then we have a friend in common."

"The badger girl."

"Now why would she have told you of my badger?"

"Yours is not the only badger in the world."

"Have you found a place for yours? I mean a place where it doesn't sort of show?"

"I paid a fellow to take it away. He was an Okinawan fellow."

"That is nice. This tastes more like peanuts than like yams, but perhaps a little more like what it looks like than either."

"Peanuts are getting to be all the thing. More and more all the thing, more and more."

"How so?"

"I am delighted with this opportunity to talk to you."

"And I with it to you."

"I know that you know that I know what you know. Therefore let us not be arch and coy."

"These are the last things I would wish to be."

"It is all going to come out anyway and you might as well be the agent as the next one. It would bring me pleasure and perhaps profit if I might help you. The dollar falls and falls and prices rise and rise, and a fellow needs more and more money if he is going to stay awhile in this pleasant vendible land. My, my. What are these little brown things at the bottom that look

141

far less like yams than like 'fermented soybeans' or mouse leavings?"

"Well, I do have a slush fund, of sorts. I must remember to call the expression to Miss Shiraito's attention."

"She says you are pithier than I am."

"I suppose the thing I want to know most at this point is how much the public prosecutors know. Have you ways of knowing?"

"Let me look into it. Off hand I think from what Harry says that they know just about everything. That is not what worries him. They will not do anything unless they have to."

"Do you have a fixed bill of fees?"

"Oh, just let me have whatever you feel you can spare and wish to give. Here are all my name cards. If one doesn't work, try the next. No, I won't need yours, thank you. I know your name, and all three of your home telephone numbers."

And why do I tell you of this, Miss Hilda Gray, way off on the range of the buffalo? Because you are the person I most enjoy confiding in, and because you more than anyone I can think of will understand what I am up to. It is not venal politicians I am interested in. They are to be found the world over, and are not interesting. I made this little request of Mr. Rooby because I want to learn the full proportions of a matter the newspapers of this land are keeping from their public, and I want my revelations to take a form that cannot be ignored by them. I want those cozy little clubs of newspaper reporters to be sorry. If they had let me be cozy with them, why then I might have behaved like a good *Flush* man, and kept the trade secrets.

> Oh a *Flush* man is a hush man,
> And he puts things on a shelf.
> Had they clubbed me and not snubbed me,
> I'd be one of them myself.

The daylight part of this Friday the Thirteenth is coming to a close, and I must go down to the lake again, and smell the lotus leaves, which are their best in the cool of evening. I am told by my almanac that under the lunar calendar this would be the Iris

Festival, when gentlemen of old, and ladies too, displayed iris roots of enormous proportions, to what must have been some effect. I have come upon this poem, by a very famous poet, in a very famous anthology, rendered by an esteemed translator:

> In addition to the medicine bag
> an iris root is hanging on my sleeve,
> which is wet with tears of memories,
> because this is the fifth of May.

Though mysterious in some of its details, is it not a pretty picture? The fifth of May is of course by the lunar calendar. I am in favor of bringing back the lunar calendar. Everything comes later, and so you have more to look forward to.

53. Miss Gray to Miss Shiraito

I feel as if I had just now caught up with the seasons, and might pick up where I left you. We were at the end of spring there, and here we are in early summer. Though this dry air is as different from the dripping air of Kyoto as air can be from air, it has the same wistfulness in it, as of leaving the best time behind.

We have had columbines, and there still are a few malingerers, up in the high glens and dells, and we have had apple blossoms, down here on the plains. No one pays much attention to the latter, and I am sad for them, and sadder at the thought of how little you Japanese have made of them, lovely blossoms though they are. You will tell me that the deliberate and leisurely way the apple tree has of blossoming makes it a less fitting symbol of evanescence, which is ever on your minds, than the cherry. And shall I tell you the real reason? The real reason is that its Chinese name renders it unfit for poetry.

> Though delightful the color, delightful the smell, it
> Is yet by its sinonym rendered invalid.

143

And also we have had plums, wild and cultivated, and of them, also, let me sing:

O odorous plum's scent –
You really are some scent!

The hints you have given of your plans for your brother and me are certainly very delicate. Products of the robust new continent, George Brown's are altogether less so. Combining this letter from him with your most recent one, I think I can surmise what those plans are.

They cannot be, my dear. They cannot be, leastways as I figure in them as a moving force, and not just a passive recipient.

I cannot keep your brother from coming to this country, and I would not be rude to him if he were to appear on my doorstep. If it were your aim to have him leave Japan permanently, then I would do what I could to help him in accommodating with us peculiar foreigners. But though I have not met him, I do not think him, somehow, the type to make his way on the wild frontier; nor do I think that this is your aim.

If I am right, then what you are suggesting can only be a postponement of accommodations that must be made before anything else can be considered. As a wise man, I forget whether of the East or of the West, observed upon an occasion, we are none of us getting younger. My views follow inexorably from this basic truth, nowhere more basic than in your country. In your country the fight to keep abreast of one's precise contemporaries begins with the nursery-school examinations and leaves off only at retirement or death, whichever comes first (unless, as I have heard to be sometimes the case, death fails to bring an end to it). Your brother has fallen quite far enough behind already. He must be pushed and pulled and shoved and knocked into joining the forward scramble. In this I think your father entirely right.

Now let us turn to another Shiraito. There continue to be signs. A couple of mornings ago there was a letter to an editor.

All piggishly, or doggishly, one of those youth communes had been raided. After objecting to what he or she (the name was withheld) judged to be the fact that the police were without a search warrant, the writer of the letter set down the sentence of most interest to us: "Anyway what difference does it make whether Shiroto was there or not and whether she had papers or not is what I say and you can tell them I told them and you too."

What caught my interest was the apparent Japaneseness of the name, and the very strong probability of a mistranscription. I doubt that any Japanese ever had the name. We both of us, you and I, know what *shiroto* means, and if there are among our readers they who do not, I may refer them to the charming entry in Kenkyusha, and particularly to a sentence offered by way of illustration: "Don't talk like a woman strange to a life of shame." As a common noun it is common, but I doubt very much that it exists as a family name. Am I right? But there is an obvious similarity to a family name which, though rare (I remember well the interesting thing you said about its incidence in the Tokyo telephone directory), does indeed exist.

That the possibly Japanese person, by being absent at the time of the raid, sent piggish fascism into a spin, from which it may or may not recover, seemed clear.

I called and asked if the full name of this person was known. Some time later, to my considerable and pleasant surprise, my call was returned, and I was given a name the family part of which matches yours perfectly and the other part could only be that of a Japanese man.

From this two conclusions emerge: 1) that in the case of the Japanese, as in the case of the turtle, it takes an expert to tell the sexes apart; and 2) that there either are now among us, or recently have been, Japanese wetbacks (do you know the expression?), among them one named Shiraito. And yes a third conclusion seems to press forward as well: 3) the Japanese in question must be young, for no one older than anyone else is ever admitted to these communes. (Are you aware of the fact that "pig" is properly "young swine"? I thought you might want to know.)

The other signs have been telephone calls and presents.

I would be upset by a series of calls in which I am breathed at and hung up on had I not had forewarning. I am sure that all are local calls. Once I said: "How is the weather down in Memphis?" There was a catching of the breath before I was hung up on. Whoever it is just wants to know that I am still here, or perhaps that I am out, and is quite without malice, I am sure.

Flowers and grasses have been left at my door. Such pretty arrangements of weeds as I have had! I am not joking. They are delightful. They suggest nostalgia, and an eye for weeds such as no American has, leastways in this part of provincial America.

Please write and assure me that you are not angry with me in the matter of your brother. My fondest regards to your father and everyone. Do you know I have never thought to ask whether the mynah bird has a name?

54. Miss Gray to Mr. Brown

Summer has come. It is the season our publicists make most of, but in fact it is a skin-parching, weatherbeating one. The fruit trees were beautiful for a time, and so were your columbines. Most of the fruit trees are imported; the columbines are native, and therefore finer, I think, braver. You can have your irrigated lands, if they are what you want. For me the dry ones, where sunflowers and other yellow things, stinking willies perhaps, do somehow manage.

> On the irrigated lands
> Are exoteric stands.
> Oh rather give to me
> The native dry-land sunflower (*Helianthus annuus*),
> columbine (*Aquilegia coerulea*), and cottonwood
> (*Populus balsimifera*) tree.

It seems utterly improbable that anything as delicately lovely as one of our purple columbines should have come into bloom in a few inches of shelter surrounded by all the wide, harsh, hostile plains; so improbable that natural selection does not seem adequate explanation.

Well, now. Well, then. You did not waste time, did you. Our local press, usually indifferent to things that come in over the mountains, which are the western limit of its world, found your articles interesting. A reason may be that one of our persons in Washington is believed to be owned by Dedlock (unless they have sold him).

It is a fine, brave story, is what I say, and had our press not noticed, the loss would have been its. I think I see the parts that come from Miss Shiraito. If she seems not to recognize them herself, it will be amusing pretense, at which she is so deft in her relations with her father. I think that perhaps you are a little hard on public prosecutors, or procurators, as the dictionaries call them, and their failure to prosecute. Back in the days when I was more interested in China than in Japan I got to know two or three of them, and thought them honest and industrious persons seeking to acquit themselves of their duties under trying circumstances, not the least of these the whims of politicians.

But of course that is secondary. You plot points along a line towards a *Flush* that does not flush very well. Has notice yet been taken by this last? And if so have the sinister five fingers, no, ten, of the C.I.A. been detected? It is only a matter of time, I am sure.

Congratulations, anyway. I will be following you eagerly each morning while the local press permits, and thereafter, similarly eager, will await reports from back east.

Now for other, less glorious things. I think I agree with you about the brother's thing.

> Yearning sooner, yearning later,
> Not for Pater, but for Mater.

And why, so good at telling a story to oodles of publics, were you not able to tell a plain, straight story to poor old Hilda Gray, who likes you? I coupled your most recent letter with

Miss Shiraito's, and a pretty couple they made, too, and added several intuitions, and they were fat, Zen-like intuitions, too; and I surmised the nature of the course being proposed for the brother. Just as not everyone can "get a grip on something with an open hand" (Mr. Mao), so not everyone could have surmised so ingeniously.

I have told Miss S. in no uncertain terms that it must not be. There is no greater uncertainty, however, than "no uncertain terms." You must tell her in no uncertain terms that there is no note, no smallest mote of a note of paradox, in these my uncertain terms, no possible glimmer of paradox whatever. The boy must be forced into action. With a hundred million Sammys on the run, how can he alone expect to stand still? Why the very people who tell us to stop and have a tea ceremony are running like mad, and making millions.

I think that the sister is probably here, withal, and probably without wherewithal. Yesterday morning there came a call. Having an intuition, because though calls of a certain kind usually come in the evening, this one, so early in the morning, had the feel of such a one – having an intuition, I say, I quickly consulted an almanac. Yes indeed: yesterday was a day when new departures may be essayed in the morning, but are to be avoided in the afternoon.

The silence was somehow different. It was expectant, pregnant.

"And is there nothing I can do for you, whoever you are?"

"Thank you for asking is there nothing I can do for you whoever you are."

"And is there?"

"No. Thank you each time."

"Where are you calling from?"

"Nashville."

This Tennessee thing: I think it may have to do with the well-known playwright, who seems to stir maternal impulses. I have noticed it elsewhere, at other times.

She was down on Broadway, of course. If I had had someone with me, I might have turned the telephone over to that person and hurried down.

"But I think I might be able to do something for you. Shouldn't you tell me your name?"

"Yes."

"Well?"

"Yes, I shouldn't."

I had done it again. Negative questions, poor dears, are caught between the hordes of the East and the hordes of the West, and doomed to extinction.

"Your family is worried. May I tell them you are well?"

"I am well. I have had no family."

"You must come here. We will have a good talk."

"What constitute your qualifications?"

It was a prepared answer. I tried no further.

The gypsy encampments have left the creek bottom and moved off to the mountains. I am very certain that the silences which you must intersperse among the above remarks were not long-distance. So she must have withdrawn from her band, or bund.

I cannot but think that there will be more in my next letter.

Or are you no longer interested in Shiraitos, now that you have had what you wanted of one of them? I will be very disappointed in you if that is the case.

How many blackheads, do you think, will roll? It seems a pity that, knowing what you knew, you did not get a corner on the headbox supply.

I am sorry that I cannot give you a pressed columbine to add to your collection. It is against the law to pluck them, though people evade the law by pulling them up by the roots. Perhaps the younger Miss Shiraito will have with her, when she comes, some roots of enormous proportions. I will give you three, my friend.

55. Miss Shiraito to Miss Gray

It is Midsummer Day, and the rains go on. Day after day, they go on. When will there be a break, that the gloom may leave our hearts, the dew our sleeves, the mildew our shoes? And "the water pipe is leaking," as a poet said in one of the best-loved of our court anthologies.

It has been such a helter-skelter day that I cannot muster myself to compose a poem, or even a translation. Let, therefore, this suffice:

> Yodo's marsh where people reap the water oat
> has swelled by rain;
> and the bright moon
> is reflected clear therein

I pause only long enough, for if these questions are not asked as they come up, they may, who knows, be lost forever, to ask whether modern English prosodic usage permits rhyming "rein" with "rain."

Such a helter-skelter day as it has been.

"My heart was in my throat," said Mr. Minawata, when it was all over.

I would flush to give you the Japanese original, pithier by a deal than any Americanism I can think of just at the moment. You will find it among the illustrative images in Kenkyusha's definition of *kintama*, which Mr. Brown says is his very favorite among all those tens of thousands of definitions. Also in the illustrative material is "grasp a person by his vulnerable spot," which will perhaps point your speculations in the right direction.

Whether Mr. Minawata was wholly taken by surprise, or whether he only meant that it had been worse than expected, I cannot, of course, be sure. I incline towards the latter interpretation. Our imported shredding machine (domestic manufacture seems to lag behind) had been uncommonly busy for some days. We have been ordered to say nothing at all of the shredding, and that is what I intend to do.

It all began at ten in the morning. As if the fact might be important, my eye descended to the clock on the Monstrous Bank, across the street. Everyone save the most distant commutors and Mr. Kuromaku was in place. Mr. Kuromaku always makes his entrance last, and does it as if reviewing the guard.

There they were on our top floor, thirteen of them, as if on purpose. I took the count immediately, because I was afraid that I might not have enough teacups. We do not often have callers in such numbers. Each wore a suit of dark blue and a tie of silvery blue. Each wore also a mildly horrified expression, as of chancing upon some foreign custom. They were like as peanuts in a pod.

Their twenty-six lips were tightly pressed together. Nothing was permitted from them. "I do not know what excuse to make," or "No words can be found to justify our barbarism," or "We do most certainly owe you a myriad of myriads of apologies," or "It is the suddenness and want of warning which make it inexcusable" – these are the things that would have come easily and made us all feel so much better.

Only this much was spoken, by the oldest of them: "Take me to your chief."

At that point in time it was Mr. Minawata. Until Mr. Kuromaku arrives each morning Mr. Minawata is his vicar, and I must say that he has a knack. All ten fingers in a bunch, he sits reading the *Wall Street Journal* as I steep him morning tea.

"You know that I am not to be disturbed," he said, turning it right side up.

"There are many," said I, making silence more eloquent than words, and steeping no tea.

Mr. Minawata came to the outer office and took a document from the senior person, him who had spoken. He held it to the light, as if searching for I know not what, and said, "I regret having put you to so much trouble so early in the day," gave a little salute, and started for the elevator.

I do not know whether, had he chosen his moment better, he would have made it. All the elevators at that moment opened, and he was swept back by a great flood of newspaper reporters and photographers; and then, let me tell you, the swill was in the fan. It was exactly three past ten by the Monstrous clock. Everything suggested delicate timing.

I said that about the swill in the fan because I learned it from Mr. Brown and like it. Actually a bomb seemed to explode with the arrival of the press, and yet the thirteen went about their business with a cold swiftness that was like a performance. I thought of a fire, and the way the firemen, shapeless lumps until a moment ago, suddenly become well-honed acrobats, taut and agile.

Two of the thirteen went for the shredder, of which they examined this facet and that and the other, and the expenditure of flash bulbs was at that moment something. The others commenced emptying drawers into maws of corrugated cardboard. More bulbs, and more and more, and then some. The reporters created a kind of roar, as of a great surge of responsibility, but it was the photographers who were really having their time, establishing, as democratic process requires, that they had been there. The Monstrous clock crept slowly clockwise.

When one of them reached my desk I thought it necessary to take a stand. I do not know why I did, in view of the fact that Mr. Minawata had done nothing to keep them out of his office or Mr. Kuromaku's. Perhaps it is my White Lily training. (Oh, in case I forget: the mynah bird's name is Susannah.)

"What can this mean, sir?" said I.

"Yes," said he. "No," giving me a little pat with one hand and a little pinch with the other, down below the line of the cameras. He seemed to be number five or so in the pecking order (as I once heard Mr. Brown call the vertical minisociety), and his eyebrows ascended into a sort of ready-made frown, giving him a more mildly horrified appearance than the others. For no reason at all, the thought crossed my mind that he would be just right for my sister. (In case I forget: will you lend return air fare?)

"What can this mean, sir?" I said again; and he pinched me again, down there below the cameras. "They are just my vocabulary lists," I said as they, and that is indeed what they were, commenced disappearing into a corrugated cardboard maw.

Then I turned to making tea. Foreseeing the need, someone had thoughtfully brought extra cups from the cafeteria. The reporters pretended that they had no time for it, and the photographers really had none.

"A good hand," said Number Five, gazing at one of my vocabulary lists. "A practiced hand. That of someone who has had practice."

I turned ninety degrees away, petulantly showing my profile.

"Very pretty." Whether he said this of my profile or of my hand, each one must judge for each one's self. Again the thought crossed my mind: you could do worse than a rising young procurator. Do you think my sister and I look alike? The thought is but one that came to me.

It had all seemed very exciting at first.

"Like the day the helicopter got mixed up," said Ms. Aobana.

A helicopter was buzzing around outside now, a *Flush* one, but it was not mixed up. The world was being informed that something was going on inside House of Craft, and that the *Flush* was on duty.

At first, I say, it was rather exciting; but as I saw my notebooks disappearing into that maw, I felt a certain slippage.

"When may I have them back again?" I asked Number Five.

"When all this torment is over."

"You promise me?"

"Who, in this world, can be certain of the morrow?"

Not only a procurator, but a procurator with a speculative, meditative bent! Perhaps I shall so humble myself as to ask my father to make inquiry as to his identity.

"Did all of you go to Tokyo University?" I asked, not wanting to be personal.

"Only twelve of us."

Though fairly certain that no one so young would have risen to Number Five if not from Tokyo University, I would have liked to ask who was the thirteenth. A procession, however, of procuratorial visages, looking grimly in place over corrugated cardboard, had just then started for the elevators. The cameras were upon us. It was their moment.

"Look agape (with wonder)," someone shouted at me, not at all softly.

I tried.

Presently all were gone, procurators and press. A hush settled over things. It was apparent to the lowest and slowest and dullest of us (do not ask me to name names) that with all those papers gone we would have trouble telling what month it was.

"We should have put every last thing into the shredder," said Mr. Kuromaku, who had just put in an appearance, having lost much dignity by being swept back into an elevator upon an earlier attempt to put one in. We had all observed, and someone, Ms. Aobana, I think, had laughed.

"Including my notebooks?" asked I, filled with woe.

"I didn't think of them, alas," said Mr. Kuromaku. "They should have headed the list."

"You do them too high an honor, sir."

"You have been of such very great service," said Mr. Minawata. "Do let me look at your notebooks, if ever they come back. I have so much to learn."

He certainly can be inscrutable at times.

So much for our morning. In the afternoon we wandered around looking in the same drawers time after time, as if hoping.

"They missed something," said Ms. Aobana.

"What?"

"The toilet paper," she said, wittily.

I must say that the place looked far neater than I had ever seen it before. You remember those little pieces of tissue paper that were everywhere, giving the place such a busy look? Yes, of course you do – Mr. Brown once said, and you agreed, that it needed raking. Well, they were gone, and everything is pristine, as if awaiting a new tenant. Expectant, as if waiting for someone to do something.

"Well, one thing," said Ms. Aobana. "Maybe now they will with more sincerity think about letting us have Saturdays off." It is Saturday, and a felicitous day for procuratorial raids.

If you see my sister, please give her my regards. I have nothing further to report of her.

Mr. Brown is well, and very much "the cock of the walk [dunghill]" (Kenkyusha). He is in all the newspapers and weekly magazines, as also is his mysterious informant, one "Deep Throat," along with a great deal of speculation as to who this last might be. The movie was so thoroughly cut when it showed here that you would have thought it about oral hygiene.

Will these rains never cease? Oh. The moon of the Thirteenth Night has just come through. Oh. It has gone again. In the air-conditioned fastnesses of Craft it is as if there were no weather. My father agrees with Mr. Brown about air conditioning, and our house here in the western marches is like a sudatorium. Mr. Brown says that air conditioning will have an effect on Japanese culture. The loss of weather (says Mr. Brown) will create a gap that anything could rush in and fill. Television (says Mr. Brown) fills its own emptiness, and that is different.

What do you think, sitting there high and dry? Oh. There it is again. I must close. Tomorrow is about to begin, and I wish this to be today's letter.

56. Mr. Brown to Miss Gray

Tonight there is a glorious full moon. This island realm does not now fix its gaze upon the moon with the intensity that is employed in autumn, when there is a chill in the air and life is receding; and yet it seems to me that on these muggy nights the full moon has the effect that a ghost is supposed to have, of making one's pores close with a great sucking sound. We are having, you see, an empty rainy season, by which is meant one without rain. It seems to be good for geraniums. And how is it for badgers? All I can tell you is that mine goes on simpering.

The fat is in the fan but for real, and I am enjoying an enormous amount of exposure: enjoying it in the sense of having it, whether or not I take pleasure in or derive satisfaction from it.

I rush from interview to interview, from channel to channel, not the asker of questions but the asked. I am a celeb. I have taken on all comers, thinking it A Novel Experience, perhaps, indeed, A Unique One. But I will (shall?) have to begin excluding certain categories. The magazines for eager students of English will have to go, because I weary of having my English corrected. I do not use "shall" and "whom" as they are used in the universities of this land. I think also that the women's magazines must go, because they intrude so upon my privacy, informing the public how often I change pajamas, and why.

In the case of magazines with thoughts of maintaining the standards professed by the haughty newspapers that own them, I believed myself to be quite the little opinion-maker until I came to have a certain sense of disjunction. One thing did not, somehow, lead to another, and I came to see that I was not really talking to anyone at all. No one is much interested in what a mynah bird says, but people are often very much interested in the fact that a mynah bird can talk.

Here is how it goes. I recreate from memory, and may make myself seem cleverer than in fact I was, and my interviewer, let us say Miss Blacktarn of "Chatterday" on Channel One, less clever. If there are details that need verifying, you might ask Miss Shiraito for her tapes.

"And now, the newest among our New Faces. Let me begin by asking a very personal question. If it seems too personal, you must forgive me, and be tolerant of the insularity that leads to such rudeness. Is your family name Brown or George? Some of those channels with larger numbers have it the former way, and some of them the latter."

"Brown. Otherwise it would be Brown George, and that

would sound funny."

"Ho, ho, ho. There is so much I want to ask you, Mr. George, and our time is so limited. I was much struck with what you said, it was five and a half years ago, on this Channel One, about Japanese tobacco."

"I don't smoke."

"You remember! Among the many things which have struck us all must be counted your quite extraordinary memory."

"Shucks."

"I beg your pardon?"

"I was speaking a European language. What I meant to say was, you are entirely too kind."

"Now that brings me to a question which was not second on my list, but which may be put there all the same. That you should say this to me suggests that you find Japanese women more interesting than Japanese men. Other things which you have said on this channel, as well as things which you have said on channels with larger numbers, have suggested the same."

"Oh yes. Oh yes indeed."

"And how does Mrs. George feel about this proclivity? Mrs. George is here in Tokyo with you, no doubt, and the several little Georges as well?"

"*Ah mais non.*"

"I beg your pardon?"

"It was European again. There is no Mrs. Brown – and as for the little Browns – don't you want to talk about my articles? Aren't you interested in my articles?"

"Here is a copy of Mr. Brown's own newspaper, which we have had flown in from Los Angeles to show to our 'Chatterday' audience. It certainly is a big newspaper, is it not, ladies and gentlemen. It looks as if it would print just about anything. And see all these pictures, a service to deprived minorities. We have so much to learn from your great country, Mr. George."

"May I look at it please? Whoever flew it in certainly took his time. I can see even from this distance – *would* you let me look at it please? – that it is a Sunday paper, and today is Saturday. Who was it flew it in? Turbulines?"

"Please, Mr. George. This is Channel One. We do not mention names. Do you sometimes read the Japanese press? I am sure you must find it difficult. So full of vocabulary and things."

"Much about it I find quite incomprehensible."

"Now *isn't* that interesting! And after all these years of study. Perhaps you could give us an amusing anecdote or two about how you have botched things comically with the Japanese language, that we may seek to make it easier for all of you who know it so much better than we do?"

"Do just let me look at that paper, if you will, please, that Sunday paper, and see if 'Deep Throat' is still showing."

"What a pity that our time is so limited. That, ladies and gentleman, was our newest New Face. Should popular demand bring you back, Mr. George, as not impossibly it will, I hope that you will be ready with amusing botches."

"Rumor last seventy-five days," they say in the tongue of this land. In the tongue of our own, we refer to a nine-day wonder. I am inclined to think that the tongue of our own is nearer the mark in the matter of my celebritydom. Yet I think that the case itself will not die. It is known here that you redheads are reading all about it and that fact is not to be ignored. The part about public prosecutors seems to pain people especially. There may be little sense in this land of personal privacy, but there is a powerful sense of corporate privacy.

> Let's talk about other things, yes let's
> Consider my balance of payments, etc.
> But please let's not, out of charity,
> Concern ourselves with my jurisp.

Miss Shiraito too has been in all the papers. Can it really be, I wonder, that she does not know?

"I want to go to America," she said meditatively two or three noontides ago, seeking to force a spoon into her Foojy House Prunella. "Will you lend me the money?"

"Dear me. Won't your Craft take you there if you wait awhile?"

"I am saving my salary and allowances for my brother."

"You want to see your sister, I suppose. But I am not sure how many beds Miss Gray has; and life on the wild frontier is pinched, frugal, and mean."

"I will take a sleeping bag. I want to see 'Deep Throat.'"

"Oh, I don't think so, really. I doubt that it would serve."

"Everyone says that we have a 'Deep Throat' in House of Craft. I want to see what they mean."

"Well, maybe I could draw you a picture."

"I see that you do not wish me to go. I withdraw my request. It was a small request."

"What is it, exactly, that everyone at Craft says?"

"We have been muzzled, forbidden to talk about it. Ms. Aobana wore a muzzle one day. Mr. Minawata said she should wear it all the time, she has such good eyes. What is your age, by the way. It keeps changing, from channel to channel."

"As also does yours, from outcry to outcry."

> (O tell us of Deep Throat. We all are so puzzl'd
> Alas, I cannot,
> For my own uvulations are gagg'd and muzzl'd
> And all, indeed, but garrott'd.)

The affairs of the other Shiraitos are not static. The cuckoo bird,

> Yearning now, at height of summer,
> Not for Popper but for Mummer,

seems to have thoughts of graduate school, although the details are not known. Everyone is persuaded that the youngest daughter is indeed in America.

Take care of yourself in this time of – whatever the crisis might be. Tornadoes? Locusts? Walls of water? The moon is beautiful, but it is a sultry night all the same. Can you think that we have the Lesser Heat to get through before we arrive at the Greater! It seems only yesterday that we were struggling through the Lesser and Greater Cold.

57. Miss Shiraito to Mr. Brown

How much longer will it rain, one asks. How much longer will it rain? Day after day the rain goes on, a bounty to them of the fields, no doubt, but a heavy burden upon the metropolitan spirit. The latter quite sinks into the mire. Hydrangeas luxuriate, but one can almost hear pelargonia crying to be taken home again.

> "Do not think," says the hydrangea,
> "Me an unimperfect stranger
>   To unintermittent rain."
> Whilst the genus pelargonic
> Cries for something Arizonic,
>   Something more like Bloemfontein.

And it does, too, and if you will consult the last volume of the botanical dictionary I left with you on the day of the loofah thing you will see why.

I may report further on my brother's thoughts of continuing education. My mother reported to me last evening, as we were down in the garden gathering things.

"Your younger older brother has made an announcement. Can you think what it is?"

Of course I could not. But I had to tell her so. It is one of her requirements, advance acknowledgment of the importance of a delayed statement.

"Why, no. What, pray, is it?"

"'I will go to beauty school and become a beautician if it is so important that I have something to do.'"

"Well for Peter's sake! He said it to Father?"

"I was there too. It was at breakfast."

I had missed breakfast, because of slippages and stoppages.

"And what," said I, looking up from *Platycodon grandiflorum*, on which were all manner of things, "did father say?"

"He arose from his chair, said 'Tcha!', and seated himself again."

"And then?" Another thing is that she must be pressed. She requires evidence of attention and interest.

"He took out a great sheaf of beauty-school literature, and *he* put it out of sight under the *Flush.* It was still under the *Flush* when breakfast was over. I peeped at it. Such faces, you never saw, and it is called beauty. Like the cover of *S.M. for the Junior Miss.*" She says these things sometimes. She belongs to a little circle of suburban housewives who exchange magazines, and can tell you a thing or two, when she is in the mood. "Whips and chains," she added, as if to refresh her memory. "Just see this millipede with a missing leg, poor thing. And such crowds of pismires as there are out in the darkness before moonrise this evening."

There has been a mysterious change in my status at Craft. I wonder if, with your nose for facets, you have noticed anything that might help explain it.

My status seems to be the one known as "eighty percent of the village." The expression signifies, in the vernacular, a situation in which one is denied commerce and intercourse.

"A cup of tea, Mr. Minawata?" I would say at first, all jollily.

"A cup of tea, if you please, Miss Aobana."

"Yes, sir. By all means. This very moment. Without fail."

This cheerful alacrity is not Ms. Aobana's usual way. She is a sardonic sort, and tea-pouring is one of her butts. She now has tea things of her own, boiler and steeper and all, and a whisk, with which she makes powdered tea at the drop of a hat. Mr. Minawata accepts it ostentatiously from her, he who once told me that it made him belch, etc.

"Where did you get these pretty tea things? From the cafeteria, or from some lending agency?" asked I, pleasantly, several times in the beginning, as if admiringly, but as a matter of fact they are mass-produced things, and the tea that comes from them must taste it.

"Another cup of tea, Mr. Minawata?"

"Oh, yes. But yes indeed. It has been *such* a long time since we had so skillfully steeped a cup of tea. The steeper before the last before the last, I almost think."

I suspect that I am being asked to resign. I cannot be dismissed. No one can. (Do you remember? You once said, wittily, that no one can be dismissed from a Japanese company except for talking to a foreigner.)

So I compile new vocabulary lists, and seek to remember old, vanished ones. I could consult a lawyer, I suppose, or the union, which, however, has just come back from the People's Republic of China, and is bemused.

Yesterday I passed Mr. Rooby, midway through the scramble intersection where you keep running into him. He does seem to spend an amount of time there. Maybe he is one of the barflies at Maxim de Paris's.

"We did well," he said, as he scrambled his way, and I mine. What can he have meant? "Harry, wherever he is, says he does not want to marry you any more," he flung over his shoulder.

I hate to think what the Lesser Heat and the Greater Heat will do to you if you continue this frantic pace, this flea-like traverse from channel to channel. I would like to think that, like me, you have lain in wait for the Moon of the Nineteenth Night. But no – there you are on Channel 41, and a most alarming color, I must say. Do, please, render my disquiet groundless.

58. Miss Shiraito to Miss Gray

How much longer will it rain, one asks. How much longer? Day after day the rain goes on, a bounty to them of the fields, perhaps, as doubtless it would be to you and the deer and the antelope, could it but be transported to you; but a heavy burden upon the spirit of the metropolis of this soggy island realm. Yet there are compensations. The scent of the orange blossoms seems more redolent in the ceaseless rain.

> The breeze brings me the orange scent,
> As I lie dozing on the floor,
> And also dreams, thus rec'mbent,
> Of one whose kindness was of yore.

I am quoting and so it is not I whom you are to envision on

the floor. The translation is my own. My poetess died about seven hundred and twenty-one years ago.

Such a celebrity as Mr. Brown has become! He must have appeared on about all the Japanese channels, and I would not be surprised if the Koreans had stolen him for a few of theirs.

He is so cute!

"Well, I don't really know about that, you know, I think, maybe. When I am a little older, you know, possibly, and have learned more about women. You must help me." And he smiles, and you smile right back, even though you know it's just a silly old telly.

It may be that my translation does not capture quite the straightforward American quality, you might say, of his modes of exposition. They seem to startle his interrogators, who move on to other topics. So too does he, for reasons altogether less clear, and with results sometimes surprising. There was an interview with Ms. Kuroike of "Chatterday," who had him more than once. My tape contains a gap. You will see how it is.

"A thing which you said, five and a half years ago, upon this same Channel One: a thing about Japanese tobacco."

"I do not smoke."

"Exactly! That, ladies and gentlemen of the Channel One audience, is what I wished to establish. I myself had to go to our videotapes for confirmation, and Mr. George [sic] remembered! The extraordinary memory, that is what"

There follows an indecent expletive, the occasion of course, for the gap.

When my tape resumes, the subject is an even more fascinating one:

"Perhaps you could give us an amusing anecdote or two having as its point the things which have happened as a result of your misuse of the Japanese language, which you know so much better than we do, which is why we must all try to make it easier for you, must we not?"

"Hand me, if you will please, that newspaper, that Sunday newspaper, that I may ascertain whether 'Deep Throat' is still showing."

Do you see how it is? I can understand why Mr. Brown's interrogators should move on to a new subject when thus startled by hin, but why he himself should do so, or intervene with an indecent expletive, just when the subject is the most interesting – I almost wonder if, in all the excitement, his buttons might not have come undone.

At House of Craft, for reasons which elude me, I am in the condition known as "eighty percent of the village." Doubtless you are familiar with it.

I do not, as a matter of principle, speak of my work to my father; but I did mention my problem at breakfast this morning, my purpose being to see whether his intelligence network might be able to contribute towards *éclairissement*.

"You are lucky you have not choked to death," he said, guffawing immoderately, as if something had suddenly amused him.

I tell you of this because the guffaw somehow intensified my feelings of isolation.

> Come, out of charity,
> And keep me company.

Yet in a strange way (everything at Craft Ie is strange these days) I do have company. There is one who represents the other twenty percent of the village, if that is what the expression means, and I must confess that I do not really know. It is Mr. Kuromaku, the president. He continues to speak to me.

"Good morning," he will say, and "Good day," sometimes getting them in reverse, with a glassy smile, and not addressing me by name.

He has that same glassy smile for everyone and everything, like the emperor receiving a throng, or the empress looking at the crown princess in those photographs. Things must not be going well for him in the procurators' offices.

Another thing my father said at breakfast: "Time runs on."

He said no more. His eye was on the fifteenth page of the *Morning Flush*. I saw afterwards that it was somewhat filled with news of collapsible lead pipes, in the hands of and at the heads of students of this and that bund. So I think his meaning was that if my sister does not come home now she is going to miss a good chance. The dogs (pigs) are quiet at the moment, but if this sort of thing goes on they will commence yelping (squealing) at students once more. Please tell her so, more or less, when you see her.

She may need money for her return passage. Something about her reticence suggests as much. We are a reticent people, and that is why, as the *Flush* keeps pointing out, we have so much trouble making the world understand.

Appeal to her with memories of home. Tell her that Susannah never ceases to talk about her. Tell her that my mother will cook the raw sea-slugs she likes best. Tell her that the orange blossoms are in bloom, reminding us and promising us – well, I do not think that they have traditionally done the latter, but we do not object to the necessary fib, if it escapes unnoticed.

Sing to her over the telephone "Home Sweet Home." If you know the Japanese version, "The Lodging in the Red Mud," so much the better.

I write to you under the Moon of the Nineteenth Night. The thought that, only a little while ago, this same moon shone upon you as the Moon of the Eighteenth Night brings a shudder as of confronting the unknowable.

59. Mr. Brown to Miss Gray

Today the Lesser Heat begins. The emptiness of this rainy season doubtless has something to do with the fact that it feels more like the Greater Heat, a fortnight ahead of us. There were those chilly days a few weeks ago, when we fell heir to air, cool and gray, from the Sea of Okhotsk. A consciousness up somewhere makes for evenness in these things.

> Oh some are chilly, some are hot. Fine.
> Feste Burg ist unser' Gott, Ein.

It is Tanabata, when the Weaver Maiden and the Herding Boy, up there, have their annual little thing.

> Be soft, be kind,
> Autumn [sic] wind.
> Oh do not flirt
> With the Weaverskirt.

I found it in one of the best-loved court anthologies.

> My eye lights upon the adjoining poem.
> The autumn wind now blows,
> And e'en the heav'nly lover must wear
> Some clothes.

Well, now. I do not know how long it has been since last I wrote. A fortnight, perhaps – and you have not done well yourself. I suppose that the newspapers have told you, in a way, of what happened, not that any of us know very well what *did* happen. I did not expect any erstwhile occupant of so extremely high a position to be approached by the procurators.

It may be said, I suppose, that I profit from the wise and lofty air of mysteriously knowing everything which the newspapers maintain. Since the whole truth does not come out, people give me credit or blame for what has happened. I am Tom Thumb the giant killer.

I go on being a celebrity, ever, indeed, more so.

It is very time consuming. I feel like the person recently referred to by one of Chairman Mao's colleagues, who is trying to catch ten fleas with ten fingers. I could merely say no, of course; but I do not expect it to last long. Nor would I wish to deny that I have found it amusing.

The sense of disjunction persists, the sense of irrelevance. Let me give you the conclusion of my most recent talk, on Channel One, with Miss Blacktarn, as I remember it.

"We must have a time of reflection, all of us, as evidence grows that external knowledge of our land is so much greater than internal. When did you first become interested in the Japanese language, the cause of these amusing blunders?"

"I have had a series of Japanese wet nurses since I was a teeny."

"A little old for a wet nurse, might one say? How does Mrs. George view the penchant?"

"She endorses it completely. When you have a wet nurse, what need have you of a wife, she is always saying."

"Stay tuned, all of you out there, to Channel One. The high point of our 'Chatterday' is just now passing, but we have as our next attraction a mynah bird that has been trained to talk exactly like Mr. George."

Miss S. is having a bad time of it, poor dear. The rest of the team, over there at Craft, is demonstrating its ability to get along without her.

What can one do? You will say that I have done quite enough already, and that it was badly done. I will reply with a parable.

Once, years ago, the chairman of a large political party was stabbed to death by an intense young person. The cameraman who won all the prizes could probably have prevented the assassination by throwing his camera at the young person. But he went on taking pictures.

Think well upon this parable.

And do not forget, in your preoccupation with the Lesser Heat, that the Greater yet lies ahead. Take potions. Is there news of the other Miss Shiraito?

60. Miss Shiraito to Mr. Brown

The rains go on. How long, one asks. How long? The maiden of ancient ages, before tea was widely taken, had nothing to occupy her time, and that is what the long rains signify in our courtly lyrical tradition.

This moonless night is that of the Double Seventh, Tanabata, the Seventh of the Seventh Month, the night of the annual meeting, so soon over, of the stars known in Japan, and in

China too, as the Cowboy and the Weaver.

> The Cowboy leaves his Weaver
> In her bower by the river,
> And somewhere cries a plover,
> Lonely for a –

Can you think of a rhyme? I cannot. The poet, a foremost one, and a literary critic as well, only suggests that there is a nameless something.

Sendai has a lovely Tanabata festival, when it is better, by the lunar calendar, under a waxing half moon. Will you go and enjoy it with me?

It being a Monday, even if not a very good one, I was at Craft early in hopes that I might find a new beginning. I did not. Things go on, for me, much the same. I keep office hours and then some, nor do I let them pass useless away. I improve myself; but the steeping and whisking of tea have been taken over entirely by Ms. Aobana. She has an easier time than I did. It may or may not be a less interesting time. Very few people come this way. Mr. Kuromaku continues to dispense his frozen smile in all the eight directions, and to spend much of his time in the offices of procurators, more, indeed, than in his own.

Little bits of tissue paper are beginning to accumulate on, in, and under desks, but not soon will our offices again have that lived-in look. The emptiness of the file cabinets seems to breed emptiness. The joy of the hunt has disappeared.

It certainly is good to see you jumping from channel to channel like a flea, or perhaps I mean a gazelle. I was at a White Lily reunion on Saturday. All of my classmates think you have the cutest accent. One or two of them professed to detect in it a trace of Sendai, and blamed me. It does not matter. You are a foreigner.

Why have you taken to telling your interviewers that you are married? Are you?

"How nice," says my mother, each time you do. "I had been worried, and I am sure that his mother was too. Do have him and Mrs. George come around some time for thick bean-meal soup with sugar and rice cake."

"Brown."

"Yes."

Even if it is true, I think you should not say it. It is not interesting. People will lose interest.

I wish I might telephone. I envision you gazing into the far heavens, waiting for the stars to meet, not knowing that they do it properly by the lunar calendar. I will telephone you.

I did not get you. Take care of yourself all the same.

61. Miss Gray to Mr. Brown

Summer has come to our high plains. The advertisements distributed among the lowlanders announce how cool it is.

> Come to (as the deer do) play,
> They say,
> And come to (as also the antelope) stay.

Only the sunflower holds out with real success against the wind that blows. It ought to be our state flower, as it is that of one of our neighbors. It has come to better terms than any other thing, save only the grasses, buffalo and grama, that puts forth leaves. The scrub oak clings to northern slopes, and the sunflower advances out into the open, and there blows. And suddenly evening comes, and it is as if the tearing and wearing and searing of the wind, all the day long, were there to make beautiful this evening hour.

> And if you come to play,
> Or if you come to stay.
> Come of even –
> > Tide. The winds
> > Their sins
> Are then forgiven.

169

Render this small lyrical effusion *a la japonaise*, and you will find that its rhymes become perfect.

The expected has at length happened, if we may turn to the business at hand.

Miss Shiraito has perhaps told you of her request that I capture her sister. Upon receiving it, I wavered between a wish to leave town and a wish to be of assistance. The latter prevailed.

In the still of yesterday evening I finally met the sister.

I had laid my plains. I had alerted the lady across the hall, a nice lady who thinks everything a lark. If I knocked on her door in a certain manner she was to emerge with all deliberate haste and come back across the hall and take charge of the telephone. I suggested that she talk about fish-gut paste, the lodging in the red mud, and other homey things.

Well, last evening the telephone had that special sound to it, and when I picked it up, that special silence. I dashed forth and knocked, and she dashed back with me, and I dashed out to my bully little Subaru and down to the telephone booth named Tennessee.

There *she* was, utterly in blue denim.

I opened the door and sought to block the way, but she was as quick and elusive as a cat. Indeed her performance was in every respect cat-like. I will not seek to defend my choice of the word. You will remember that I am a cat lover.

In a trice she was speeding down the street. I was after her, not expecting to catch her, wanting only to see where she might speed. I did in fact catch her. Have you ever seen a cat pursued by a dog when there is no tree to climb? It initially springs far into the lead, and manages to stay there for a few hundred yards, but it tires, and is had. So it was with us. To my very considerable surprise, I found that I was at her side. Perhaps she wished to be overtaken. I cannot say.

Her behavior continued to be cat-like. She sort of spat at me and made flailing gestures, as if she meant to use her nails.

I introduced myself. That seemed the polite thing to do.

"I don't know," she spat. "I don't know."

I suggested that we shift over to Japanese, in which such expressions as "I don't know," coming from so much further forward in the mouth, are so much more spittable. They are the expressions a babe learns to spit with its mother's milk.

She flailed again, and across a brief portion of its trajectory one of her nails did in fact catch my cheek.

Then she was quiet. A spitting kitten will suddenly change its mind and roll over to have its stomach tickled. She started back in the direction whence we had come. If I was not already bleeding I was soon afterwards. The doctor said that he had seen many a man thus scratched up, but never a woman.

That is how I made the capture. We were soon in my Subaru, and, after a quick trip to the infirmary, back in my apartment.

"Absolutely delicious," the lady across the hall was saying. "I do not see how you could tear yourself away."

Apparently Miss S. had neglected to hang up. The telephone company of your island realm would long before have cut short a call from a pay telephone.

I have her with me. She was silent at first. She used only two words, "yes" and "no," and only in answer to questions. From them I put together the outlines of the story, which are as we had imagined them to be. She left Japan with a false passport, in the company of other members of her "bund." The date would seem to be that averred by her father's kindergarten intimate. Through some underground railroad they attached themselves to one of the bunds that wander, and wandered. She withdrew in the spring, intending to come to me. You will see, therefore, that although I got wounded in the process, I cannot claim that it required any great ingenuity on my part to make the capture. It is true, of course, that not just everyone would have thought of fishgut paste and – what was that other?

Early this morning I asked whether she meant to rejoin them.

"By no means. No. On no account."

These expressions, from *our* dictionary, marked the break-through. The effect was as of a triad, a divine monosyllable flanked by guardians.

As I dated this letter, I noted for the first time that yesterday, the day of the capture, was the thirteenth; and I was moved to look in my almanac for further information about it. An uncommon sort of day it was, too, a confluence of the bad points on more than one cycle. We stayed up most of the night, she and I, she giving monosyllabic answers to my questions; and indeed it was the vigil of the Brazen Monkey, that one night in sixty when my Kyoto landlady and her friends stay up all night. I wonder if she knew.

"Take me to church," she said this morning.

It is Monday, but I found in the yellow pages a Catholic church with something on, and, since she specified no denomination, Catholic or heathen, we went. She put a kerchief over her head, White Lily fashion.

"What do you mean to do now?" I asked as we were at post-recessional coffee.

"I have a wish to go to Disneyland."

"Do you not think of going back to Japan?"

"No."

I quickly saw what I was doing. "Do you think of going back to Japan?"

"That is beyond dispute."

"Then you must go very soon. Immediately. There will be other times for Disneyland. I am sure that your father will be more than happy to take you, once he has you back. This is a time for firmness and decision. When can you be ready?"

"At the earliest practical moment."

I called immediately for reservations, and enclose the schedule made out by the travel agent. The thing which happens to illegal immigrants is they get deported if and when caught. I do not know the thing which happens to them who knowingly give aid to illegal immigrants. The matter was of some urgency. Thus do I seek to justify what I have done, though it may seem that I took unfair advantage of a Kenkyushaism.

She listened as I made the reservations, and afterwards said, "You have stood me in good stead in my time of need."

She said it with a sad little smile. I fell silent, composing. Kenkyusha does that to me.

"You have stood me in stead in my time of need,"
> Said she to her.
"On, no, I demur,"
> To she said her.
"I have stood instead of the one who indeed
Should be standing in stead, in this time of need.
I wish you godspeed
In this time of need,"
> To she said her.

I am glad I have a little money in the bank. Her list of phrases does not seem to include matters of credit and interest. I suppose she thought it unnecessary to be armed with them.

I asked about the masculine name reported to me at the time of the raid on the commune.

"He is an odious fellow. He is abhorrent to my feelings."

She said it with much spirit, as if she hoped that he had gone to the pigs, but for the most part she is as pure a White Lily as you could hope to meet. The sisters look very much alike. This one is a little rounder, and for the most part wears on her countenance a blank serenity that makes it difficult to imagine her as one of the girls in the bund.

She has spoken again. "I must go and purchase some souvenirs of my stay abroad. Some things which will form (make) good (fitting) souvenirs for my home friends."

And she took out a little paper purse that folds shut and needs no clasp, a most ingenious product of the land of paper folding. From it she took fifty dollars so new that they might have come from a bank robbery. Perhaps, who knows, they did.

She could not go home without presents. Thus are the deeper ways of the tribe respected by its delinquents.

I will close, therefore, and we will go down town and buy some gimcrackery imported from Japan.

I will not write to our Miss Shiraito (probably the only person in all monstrous Tokyo who at this moment bears that name, unless, and I do not remember, the baby out in the garden closet is the right sex). I leave the enclosure to your discretion. I do not want to be involved with old kindergarten friends. If there is no one to meet the younger Miss S. at Haneda Airport, she can take a cab home, and her father can clean up the aftermath. If there are immigration persons, he can do the same, though the strain will be greater, perhaps, upon the bonds of friendship.

As for your celebritydom, well, that is about it, as the younger Miss Shiraito said not long ago, in response to something. The remark must lie buried somewhere or other in Kenkyusha, a rendition of something or other, and you and I will come upon it at some time or other. (I am quite filled with thoughts of things.) I had a brief twinge of provincial celebrity-dom myself, down in Kyoto once, and the recollection of it gives me an idea for making yourself more interesting. Why don't you, when they have you talking like a mynah bird, talk like a female mynah bird? I am sure it would make the celebritydom last longer, and you might find your world broadening to include a few sexes of whose existence you had not dreamed. Even its detractors admit that Tokyo has a great many sexes.

In the matter that is the cause of it, your celebrityhood, I think you are being too modest. The Eastern press gives you entire credit for what has happened, including the procuratorial interview with the erstwhile person. Our own press is again landlocked, concerned only with what it calls its Mountain Empire, despite the fact that a good eighty percent of us live out here on the plains.

It has been my experience that this time when the Lesser Heat is giving way to the Greater is a most trying time for man, woman, and priest. Do you not think that you should take a vacation, and tell Miss Blacktarn that you will be back at the Time of the White Dew? But no, you cannot. Who is this man, she will say, who comes to me in the Time of the White Dew, alleging promises made in the Time of the Lesser Heat? No, stay with it while it lasts, and be sure that there is one who longs to hear all about it.

62. Miss Shiraito to Miss Gray

When will they end, one said of the rains. They have ended, and now comes this heat. It will be, so they say, heat such as we have not had these many years. Already the air is heavy and still. Were I to give in to sudden, recurrent impulse and throw off these hot clothes, I would be as if swimming. I am already, only with clothes on.

> The summer moon shines upon those
> Who feel cooler in light clothes.

It is said, sometimes, that Japanese suffers from the absence of relative pronouns. I think, sometimes, looking at this and that translation from the anthologies, of which this is an example, that it benefits.

Doubtless the postal system, with its contradictions, can be blamed for the fact that we had no advance warning of my sister's return.

Yesterday evening, as I sat waiting for something felicitous to happen, there came a ringing of the telephone. It was too much to expect that it might be from you, across the sea, or Mr. Brown, off in the northeastern quarter of the city, and so I lifted the telephone, reconciled to the fact that it would not be the *most* felicitous of calls, but expecting something along that line all the same. It was from the immigration office at Haneda Airport.

Was this the house of Shiraito? Even so. Was it, then, the house of one Shiraito Momoko, also known as Susannah? Now I have told you, I believe, that the frequency of Shiraito in the Tokyo telephone directory is exactly that of the name of the professor we are always talking about. It follows that unless certain Shiraitos are without telephones, which they would hardly be, save in the farther provinces, then all the Shiraitos of Tokyo must be under one roof, or one roof and a garden cottage (with extension). It was, in brief, the silly sort of question that comes from the bureaucracy. I took the measure of it immediately.

175

"Even so," I said, with haughtiness. "She is out this evening."

"It is required that the person of responsibility in the Shiraito household come immediately to Haneda Airport in the matter of taking cognizance of Miss Shiraito Momoko, also known as Susannah."

"To whom do you have reference?"

"To the person whose name is entered in that portion of the family register designated for the name of the person known for reasons described in the domestic code as the head of the family."

"Well just imagine it in this day and age. The ward office is closed at this hour, but perhaps, if it is important, I can make inquiry at a reasonable hour of the morning as to the person of authority to whom you have reference."

"Oh stop it," said my mother, taking the telephone from me, somewhat roughly. "I am very sorry," she said, when the authoritarian demand had been repeated, "but he is out this evening. Will anyone else do?"

The answer took a little while, but the main thrust of it was clearly negative.

We three looked at one another, my mother and my older younger brother and I. The second mentioned has of late been spending his evenings at home. The other two of us know full well that this fact is not unrelated to the movements of my father, who has been absent for a number of evenings.

The first mentioned withdrew to the kitchen, and was heard addressing the mynah bird in tones more than adequate to rouse it from its dreams. The mynah bird serves the purpose a baby does in many households, to shield people from one another.

"'Nothing could be finer than to have a little mynah,'" I hummed to myself, looking at my brother, who picked up the telephone.

"Is he there?" The Japanese original was one word shorter, and contained no pronoun. Why *will* people think that Japanese is a wordy language.

He was.

176

"Momoko is at Haneda," said my brother without preliminaries. "The indications are that your presence is required."

He said nothing further, and apparently nothing further was asked.

"I too will go to Haneda," said I, getting into my shoes, and not thinking it necessary to inquire as to my father's response. The conversation, if such it can be called, had a certain thing about it.

"I will not," said my brother, getting into his shoes. Once again his movements and my father's did not seem unrelated.

"Do you think you ought to?" said my mother, it was not clear to which of us. "Will you be home for breakfast?"

How should I know? And she never knows how many people will turn up for breakfast in any case until they do so. Once I was in the cab and on my way, it came to me that possibly she wanted to go to the airport too. Else why would she have asked such a pointless question? It had not occurred to me that a female child would make her consider so long a journey. You know how far the airport is from these western marches. (And if the capitalists have their way and the new airport is one day made to function, it will be still farther.)

The immigration paddock at the airport reminded me of – shall I tell you what it reminded me of? – yes, for you, an American, will understand – a public convenience. That is how smelly it was, and how crowded it was with people who seemed to have business, and people who seemed to be passing the time of day, etc.

At first I did not attempt to go beyond the guard point. Because I was afraid, you will ask. No. Because I felt that we were here, and they were there, people and non-people. "We must unite with the masses. The more of the masses we unite with the better."

I surveyed the scene through windows and doors, picking out, among the throngs, an interrogation here, an inquisition there, an investigation in yet a third place. Among the recipients of these were Koreans, but no foreigners. Though I was too far away to take in olfactory evidence of a Korean, I could tell by reading lips, albeit I am not the lip reader I was back before tape recorders.

It was the hour when the jumbos come in. If I was to get inside, no better hour seemed at hand. A cluster of Korean types was led past, in the direction of the departure gates. They seemed to be taking the matter professionally. A couple of media types were following them, and then turned about again.

"Yes," said one of them, to the other. "My feeling exactly. We'll have a drink, and talk it over. We'll borrow some money, to do it with."

"We wouldn't want it to get into the papers, now would we," said the other, with a mass-media laugh. You know the kind.

I put my slight, petite self between them, and we three proceeded past the guard point, they unchallenged, I unnoticed. They were big media types.

Behind a pillar and some throngs, not visible from my earlier vantage point, were my father and sister. You have been feeding my sister too well.

It was up to them that my companions (so to speak) proceeded. The last remark above was repeated by one of them as we drew near, with the laugh reduced to a snigger.

"Do you have anything smaller, sir?" said the other, laying out a thousand-yen note before my father and smoothing the wrinkles. "The change machine does not seem to be working."

"Oh, but of course," said my father, handing him a ten-thousand-yen note.

"I wonder if I *too* might trouble you. A person does sometimes get caught without change."

They bowed and departed, unchallenged once more. I will not be surprised if sometimes they are confused as to which side they belong on.

My father turned again to the inquisitor, who had been as if not present at this little transaction.

"I was there myself," said my father, "but a long time before the Russians came in. How long did they have you in Siberia?"

"Four years," said the man, who was about the right age. "Long enough to get through college."

"Under the new system."

"More than enough under the old. That is where the spring-tide of my life went."

"A dirty crying shame."

Well I never! I almost said it aloud. The absence of feelings of war guilt among people of this age is perfectly astonishing!

The conversation went on for some time. My father made very skillful use of the fact that he had not been in military service himself to bring in the names of friends who had. There were some well-known names, including a war criminal or two, and the assistant chief of police with whom my father attended kindergarten in Sendai. He was extremely clever at obliquitously accounting for his civilian status, making it seem that he had been engaged in intelligence work, and might perhaps still be, against (who else?) the Russians. (I do not deny that he has a certain clever cunning.)

"Man for man you were better than they. But it was hopeless."

"It was hopeless. Someone should have told us, and given us time to get away."

"I think they knew that you were better. In fact I know that they knew it. There are documents."

"Yes, I do not doubt it."

At another time I would have had things to say about this utterly self-centered view of things. More than once, indeed, I was on the point of getting in a word for all those widows and mothers. But there was a smoothness about the dialogue that did not lend itself to the troika approach. Besides, I was watching my sister, whose (yes, you have been feeding her too well) solidity had an effect on me. She was drawing a picture of a very strange garden, lilies interspersed among cacti, or vice versa. It would not have been easy to say whether or not she was attending to the dialogue. I rhymed as I mused upon it, listening and not listening.

> I liliaceous cactaceous plot.
> A lovesome thing, this plot, God wot.

But what, peradventure, signify
Cactaceae, liliaceae?

"I think they knew it. That may be among the reasons why they kept us so long. And we were much better workers than they were, too. We built a few cities for them, here and there in Siberia. I sometimes wonder what it says about Socialism."

"And well you might. And well you might."

"Do you suppose I might have the loan of your seal for a moment?"

My father handed it to him, and he affixed it to numerous documents. Now the great advantage of our system of seals is that it gives rise to feelings of trust. You hand a person your seal, and you do not get within reading distance of the documents to which he affixes it; and this gives rise to feelings of warmth and trust.

"There should be no need for you to go out of the house," he said to my sister, as if tacking her on to the end of an otherwise interesting conversation, "until the autumn term begins, or until you are summoned, whichever is first."

"Yes," she said, in a very small voice.

And so we were all home well before breakfast, except my brother.

"We have put you to a great deal of trouble," said my father to my sister, as we got into the cab.

"Not at all," said my sister, in that same small voice.

Whereupon the generation gap took over.

My sister has kept to her room. We are likely to hear more from you about her little boondoggle than from her. My father stays in the house, and spends a good deal of his time on the telephone. Experience has demonstrated that until he sets forth again my brother will not be back.

From my sister's room come sounds of a rending of cambric, poplin, and huckabuck. She says thanks. She will, she says, write.

"How nice," said my father just now. It is not often that he unbends to such a degree.

And the voice of the mynah bird is heard. "I am happy as a skylark."

I cannot help thinking that my brother, over east of the river, is happy too.

All of which goes to show that you never can tell. The omens for the day, in every authority I have consulted, are bad ones. You never can tell, though often you can.

The moon of the Thirteenth Night is high, and looking warm, even febrile. I envy you on your side of the dateline, where the Greater Heat is slower to come. Do everything you possibly can, I beseech you, to withstand its depredations.

63. Miss Shiraito to Mr. Brown

It is difficult to endure the heat, heat such as we have not had these decades and decades, if memory serves. Beneath the leaves of the lotus, and there only, resides coolth. The shrilling of the cicadas seems more insistent as darkness advances to enfold them.

> The rains they will not stay,
> Upon this summer day,
> And in the mountain's shade is
> An uproar of cicadas,
> And in the mountains' valley
> A clamor of cicale.

I like the mysterious quality of this poem, from one of the anthologies, the leaving of something to surmise, as if it were raining and not raining, not raining and raining.

I have news, something to interest even an eminent newsmaker like yourself, which is something: my sister has come home. We got her through customs on Sunday night, as if she were in bulk, which in a way she was. Professor Gray knew of her return. We know that she knew, because of red rocks every

181

which way on those badly wrapped parcels. We do not mind. Probably it was better that we appear at the airport wearing on our visages that grimly surprised look. Yet it would have been nice if she had told us.

My sister has been silent. We may surmise that Professor Gray saw her to the airport, most competently, on wheels.

To queries as to how she found things there on the high plains, she replies: "Dusty."

To queries as to where all she has been, she makes reply in English, as if to demonstrate how far she has pulled ahead of the rest of us in that regard: "Hither, thither, and yon."

If we are to go by her gifts, which she distributed yesterday in silence, she was in places where ample measures of this and that are needed to turn back the assaults of the sun. But of course this evidence is not conclusive. The search for gifts is always rendered difficult by the need to find things which are ample and not to be found in the Mitsukoshi. I do not think that she did badly, all things considered, though one might have wished for more specific things, pennants and ashtrays and picture albums and the like. Everything has that Western look, that OK Corral look, beyond which not much can be said.

My mother tells me that my sister stayed in her own room through most of yesterday, and that there were sounds of riving and rending behind her closed door. This last my mother took as evidence of a wish for privacy, of which she had not enough in America.

"What with everybody out in the saddle all the time."

Thinking my mother's conclusion too hasty I raised a curtain a little while ago, the window being open, and asked if I might be of assistance with whatever she was doing.

What she was doing was destroying pink. Like all creative young people, she had decorated her own room, and her overwhelming preference, which indeed had excluded all else, had been for reds of low saturation. All of them now were going, all of them.

"No thank you. Unless you feel like buying a few more garbage cans."

"Why are you doing this thing?"

"Someone must."

Do you have extra garbage cans? It occurs to me that you might, since you are always saying that we Japanese are so wasteful.

My father has been at home, and on the telephone a great deal.

Sometimes, absently, doing it and not doing it, I will pick up the telephone in the kitchen, and he will be saying: "Tomorrow at four then. It was extremely rude of me to bother you by telephone. I will not seek to apologize, for my efforts would be doomed to inadequacy." Then, the other person, always a man, having hung up, he will add: "That you, Susannah? You have to be up earlier than that if you want to catch the worm."

Now really! Susannah is a clever bird, but there are limits.

My mother is calm and placid. She watches my father carefully, and seems to have been informed, verbally or otherwise, that there will be no upheavals for a time. I always catch my father at the same point in his conversations. Perhaps fate accounts for it.

He appears pleased with the results of his endeavors. This morning at breakfast he was positively gabby.

"Well, here we are. How different from a fortnight ago. Then it was sons who seemed to be present in too large supply."

"Where are they?" asked my sister, as if she had only just then thought of them.

"Oh, off in the same direction as His Majesty, I should imagine," said my father, with the insouciant diffuseness that indicates certain and precise knowledge. He had turned to the *Morning Flush*. "Here is a relevant thing. You can always count on the *Flush* to give you a relevant thing or two with your breakfast. It says that there is a boom in arranged marriages. Now that is very nice, certainly, the better sort of relevant thing. I have never understood, of course, why these things always have to come in booms. What about the children, poor things?"

"Yes," said my sister, in English. "Very."

183

"And will it be the arranged kind for you, my young persons?"

"Yes, very."

I looked at her, wondering whether she meant it, or was just being international some more. If the former, why here was a change indeed! I could see in it something akin to the disappearance of hues from her room.

"There will be time, there will be time. In the case of one who is not with us, the one-too-many of other breakfasts, time runs on, rapidly on. You might tell him so when next you see him. It will be this evening. He will be home this evening, for I will not."

I thought of asking which of his four-o'clock appointments he meant to keep.

"I hope he is getting plenty of protein and vitamins," said my mother.

"All he deserves, I am sure."

"Who is to say what he deserves?" queried I, being fair.

"Did they give you plenty of proteins and vitamins in America?"

"Yes, very."

"Go to China next time. That is where they feed you. And then some."

"'The road has twists and turns,'" said I, quoting, and departing. I had work to do.

You may think upon reference to your file of my recent letters that this is but a way of speaking. It is not. There has been a change at House of Craft, and I am back at the manifold tasks that were mine of yore. It came yesterday. Mr. Kuromaku awoke, so to speak. He had been coming in at inscrutable hours, looking like a sleepwalker who has heard a good one. Yesterday he appeared at something not far from the average of the old hours.

"Let us pass a sponge over the past," he said, with solemnity, "to a man."

Mr. Minawata, who is a lackey in good things as in bad, immediately commenced sponging. "Please continue to remember me," he said, addressing me. "I think possibly the steeping was prolonged a few seconds more than absolutely necessary," he said, not rejecting my cup of tea, and taking it seriously.

So perhaps the time has come for me to resign. I think I can do it now without loss of countenance.

I continue to have spells of dizziness and vertigo as I observe your channel-hopping. I may say, and I know that you will take it in good part, that I did not entirely like what you said on Channel 47 last night about Chairman Mao. It seemed somewhat personal, though it is true that one cannot tell about an old man. I was not at all surprised that your interviewer quickly changed the subject.

I fear I will not sleep, of such intensity is the heat. Even the moon, so near full, seems to pulse and throb. The breeze has fallen away, and the brook seems to lie still, vanquished by the heat.

> This deathlike pause.
> The breeze is not the blower,
> Nor yet the brook the flower
> That it was.

64. Miss Shiraito to Mr. Brown

The Greater Heat is true to its name. This morning it seems to overpower all the sounds of the city. I was up very early, to await the popping of the first lotus blossom. Pop it did, and the sound was not lost, among all those others. There are they who assert that the opening of the lotus blossom is as silent as silence itself, but they are wrong. The lotus leaves, covered with dew, are as if only they were exempt from the heat. As was observed in an early anthology:

> It ventures to deceive,
> The lotus leaf

185

It says these things are jew-
Els which are dew.

The full moon is just setting, this morn of the Sixteenth Day,
and the light in the east and the light in the west, catching the
dew after photochemical infraction, tell us that it will be
another blazing day.

I thought it fitting to confirm the restoration of good graces at
Craft by taking yesterday off, but to take two days off in a row
would have the effect of a premature announcement.

I did have a good excuse yesterday, having, as you know, had
little sleep the night before. Was not the moon just as in my
letter, which should by now have reached you?

I certainly was glad, having set restlessly forth and let my
footsteps take me where they would, to find you at home.

Knowing how busy you are, I wanted our hours together to
be spent efficiently. I therefore picked up where I had left off in
my letter. I had from time to time a certain sense of cross
purposes. That is all right. It is when you are unaware of cross
purposes that they are dangerous. Having received my letter,
you will see the cause of the confusion. It was not myself I was
referring to in the matter of the arranged marriage, but my
sister!

"I could not approve more warmly," you said more than
once, "for so many reasons. Traditions were put together by far
more experience than you or I will ever have."

Well, thank you very much. Some might not, of course, agree
with you.

I was at home yesterday, as I may have said. My father was in
and out. Idly picking up the kitchen telephone from time to
time, I kept finding that I would not have been able to call you.
For he has continued to telephone most busily. There has been
a change in the thrust and import of what I hear. I no longer
seem to find myself always at the end of a conversation. I think
the new subject matter may be of a sort for which he does not
mind having an audience.

At one point I heard him reserving tickets for "The Rape of

Okinawa," which is playing at Shimbashi, with the Helen Hayes of Japan in the title role. It is not the sort of thing he would be inclined to attend unless there were an occasion. I was not much puzzled to know what, this time, the occasion might be.

"That other Miss Shiraito has written another letter to the *Flush*," he said at breakfast, from which I have just returned. "She must have sent it special delivery, or hand-carried it. She has certain remarks to make about International Women's Year, and in the course of them asserts that arranged marriages are a vestige of many evil things, chief and foremost among them paternal tyranny, which has not yet been stamped out, for which reason we must go on vigorously stamping. I wonder what sort of family she comes from. No father I know of would be silly enough to insist these days, in the case of a daughter."

In the morning's *Flush* you will find, if you are interested (and I sometimes think that you are not so very interested), the letter which was the occasion for this jollity. The age is my correct one. I had not published it, because I had not wanted people to know that I was born in the Year of the Tiger; but why should you not know?

"You are all to keep this date open," said my father, displaying a great sheaf of tickets. "Momoko will tell you why, if you have any questions. Though I doubt that there is one among you who, listening and not listening, has not grasped the reason."

"Whom is the eleventh one for?" said I, counting.

"Your grandmother is coming from Sendai. I thought you knew. I called her last night, and left a persuasive message when she refused to come to the telephone."

"And the fourteenth?" asked I, continuing my count. "Younger older brother?"

"Why no. The 'all' in my last speech but one was meant to include you. Do not think, however, that I have forgotten your younger older brother. When one problem seems to be solving itself with unexpected alacrity, the time seems right for addressing oneself to the next."

And now begin the waning phases of the moon. When it

commences to wax once more, we will be at the end of the Greater Heat, and the Advent of Autumn. And where will we be in other respects? The thought of the despatch with which my father is arranging my sister's affairs and turning to my brother's intensifies yet further – one would not have thought it possible – the gray of the forebodings.

How is your lotus? A lotus is among the flora for which one can only hope.

For you, my hope is that you take care of yourself in this most trying time. I do not know by whose design it is that you are appearing on fewer channels, but think it a good design. Gather your strength in the hot weather as does the *Lycoris radiata*, "the flower of the farther shore," and spring upwards into the light when autumn comes.

65. Miss Shiraito to Miss Gray

We are in the time of most intense heat. Loud is the shrilling of cicadas, and of frogs.

> Upon a wattled gate a
>> Western sun I see,
> And hear a near cicada,
>> Shrilling lonelily,
>> Perched upon a tree,
>> Upon a tree nearby.

Actually it is morning; but "eastern" would not work well, and I would not wish to disturb the imagery, from one of the anthologies.

Do you have lotuses in Redrock? Do you like them? Is it a thing of all Americans or only of Mr. Brown, to dislike them? He recently threatened to drop his on a passing policeman.

I would not have thought it possible for one so militant as my sister to become so suddenly docile. I wonder if you Americans are responsible. Did you fail to tell her what made America great, and to offer living example? If so, I am filled with rue.

No amount of rue, however, can have much effect upon what has happened. My sister has been one of the two principal parties to a *miai*, an interview with a view to marriage; one of the principals, that is, if you leave out of your calculations my father and his; and she has accepted, conditionally only on her being allowed to live far from the madding crowd and join the P.T.A..

There we all were, in one long row, at "The Rape of Okinawa." There we all were, from left to right, or, from the vantage point of the Helen Hayes of Japan, who could not have conveyed the Okinawa thing more vividly, from right to left, his sister, the wife of his oldest brother, his mother, his paternal grandmother, his oldest brother, his father, he, she (my sister), my father, my oldest brother, my paternal grandmother (who was not pleased at having to come from Sendai for a thing having to do with a granddaughter, but did), my mother, my sister-in-law, and I.

It was the *miai*, of course. The betrothal is as good as final, though the private detectives have yet to do their work, and it is possible that their revelations will jar my sister from her insanity.

He (my sister's all-but-betrothed) put me in mind somehow of a dancing master, of one of those slithering schools: you know, the kind that makes it seem that the means of propulsion is in the spine and not the legs. Even his facial expression, or rather, the absence of expression save for a faint pursing of the lips, made me think of a dancing master. I wanted to reach up the line and determine whether cosmetics might in part account for the extraordinary fairness of complexion.

During the long intermission we all gathered in the restaurant for a modest repast. He and she (my sister) said almost nothing, and scarcely looked at each other, and what might have been the evidence upon which their mutual approval is based, I would certainly be hard put to say. In the great narrative tradition of our land, a glimpse of a sleeve is enough to stir

189

uncontrollable passions. It may have been something of the sort – not that anything especially uncontrollable was in evidence. He is a product of the Year of the Tiger, but seems altogether more like the Year of the Cow, of which we may assume that, in a more elemental sense, he is the product. My sister, you may have guessed, was born in the Year of the Sheep. (Mr. Brown is a Chicken. What are you?)

My father and his did almost all the talking. My father is, with my sister, the one who surprises me. He prefers more typical tiger types, and that he should approve suggests, well, any port in a storm. Anything will do, provided only that it does so promptly.

"And how long were you in Europe, Mr. Irokenai?"

"Two years, about, more or less."

"Two years exactly, from Empire Day to Empire Day." It was his father, and he used the old feudal word for the day. That sort of thing may help to account for my father's approbation.

Your birthday and Mr. Brown's! If one chose, one could see in such a coincidence a bond from a former life; but in this case I do not choose, I think.

"How long ago would that have been?" All of this is information which the detectives will expeditiously provide.

"What Mr. Brown calls small talk," said I to myself.

"Several years ago."

"It was a year after he took his degree from the Law Faculty of Tokyo University."

"You went on company business, I suppose?"

"Company business? You speak about company business?"

"It was a graduation present."

"Almost a year after he graduated? That added to the pleasure, I am sure. These things are so much better when you have time to look forward to them, and get ready for them. How nice that his company was willing to let him go, after having had the use of his valuable services for such a short time."

It was more than small talk. He was putting them on the

190

defensive, and I must say that he was doing it well.

"I think we should be quite frank in these matters. Do you not agree? He had resigned his first position because of a minor disagreement over mahjong and golf, and was waiting for new possibilities to open up, as they were certain to do, given his background. (I do believe in frankness at such times.) It seemed a good opportunity to go abroad and improve his English, French, German, Spanish, Italian, etc. Have you been abroad, Miss Shiraito?"

"I agree with you wholly and completely in the matter of the need for frankness. My daughter is a very traditional girl. Does she look – I ask the question in confidence that I will have a very frank answer – does she look like the sort of girl who has been abroad?"

My sister certainly did, at that point, look demure and traditional.

I think probably my father expects to bribe the detectives. He will have no trouble learning which agency has accepted the assignment. He has good connections among the detectives, from his student days, kindergarten and after, and also from his days of freely roving the continent.

I may draw the curtain upon this scene, and move on to a matter of more concern. At several breakfasts, and in almost the same words, my father has said: "I most certainly would not wish you to think, in all the excitement, that I have forgotten Younger Older Brother. When one problem seems to be solving itself with remarkable despatch, the time seems right to address oneself to the next."

The fact that my brother and my father are both at home intensifies the ominous miasma hanging over these words. The place whither my brother has been going to avoid my father, and whence he has been coming to do the same, would seem to be no longer available to him.

You were so *very* good to my sister.

Mr. Brown has commenced showing a certain tendency towards impatience, as you may have guessed from the lotus incident. There he is on Channel One again. Let me give you the interview as it devolves, that you may have a sense of immediate intimacy.

"But you are so young," says Ms. Kuroike.

"I once made someone very angry by saying exactly that to him."

"Fancy! Very angry! Foreigners have such intense feelings in these matters, and make them so abundantly clear. That is what we like about them."

"It was a Japanese person, and a famous one. You have interviewed him on this 'Chatterday.' He wrote an article about me entitled 'Yankee Go Home.' He did not mention me by name, but that I was the Yankee, there could be no doubt. So be careful about saying to a Japanese what you have just said to me."

"Thank you for your valuable advice. I am sure that all of you out on the air waves have found it every bit as valuable as, at this moment, have I. And when will you be coming again?"

"I beg your pardon?"

"You have just said that you are going home."

"Oh come, out of charity."

"I am sure all of you out there understood this last remark (which was in English); but suppose we take a small measure of precaution, if you please, Mr. George, and translate."

But with an "It is untranslatable," he now changes the subject. "How old are *you*?" he has just said. In such ways his impatience shows.

It shows too, or perhaps inattention is what shows, in such limited intercourse as I have with him. We seem ever more at cross purposes.

> What to me does this does that to him betoken.
> Perchance it would be better were the dialogúe broken?

I do not think that Ms. Kuroike really misunderstood him in the matter of his going home. Rumors are widespread, and she was contributing her bit. I have not brought the matter up, nor has he.

No leaf stirs, everything if as if shot dead by the heat, which is like molten liquid, ever more so as the day progresses. (My brother has read your descriptions of Redrock evenings, and evinced envy, both that you should have such evenings to describe, and that you should describe them so well.) Yet there is already, somehow, a premonition of autumn in the air. An old bit of moon hangs in the sky. With the coming of the new moon, autumn will be held to have begun.

> It must be cool on one side of the street,
> Where summer and autumn *en passant* meet.

This last summer poem in the first of our court anthologies makes something whimsical out of something wistful, as we are wont to do, and accords well with my own thoughts of things.

Doubtless you look exuberantly ahead to autumn as a new beginning. I hope that in your exuberance you do not overtax yourself. Please keep in mind also that the change of seasons is a time when one does well to expect the unexpected.

66. Miss Gray to Mr. Brown

Out on the plains the Indian paintbrushes are in bloom, dots of vermillion against the brown of the grasses. It is a lovely flower, the Indian paintbrush. Like the columbine, it persuades me that evolution is not the only explanation. Something else accounts for the beauty of harsh, high, windswept plains.

Late summer, when even summer school is fading away, is a time when we Look Ahead. We do not think much any more about educational reform, as we were forced to (leastways forced to pretend to) back in those days. We think rather about money, and about committees. I do not have much to do with the former, being neither a provost nor a dean. But as regards the latter – "Whenever problems arise, call a meeting." Chairman Mao would have made a model dean. "The companies . . . must hold big and small meetings of various kinds. . . . When the fighting lasts several days, several such meetings should be held." It is a brilliant description of the academic life.

Now, as to Miss Shiraito and you:

> Oh what is the matter with Mr. Brown,
>   That he does not like the lotus?
> I almost thought he would knock me down,
>   If worthy, indeed, of his notice.
> What *is* this Brown thing, pray Miss Gray?
>   I haven't the remotest.

It is the way of our people to make something whimsical out of something wistful, of something, indeed, disturbing. (I think the frontier may have something to do with the matter.) I enclose a copy of Miss Shiraito's most recent letter, which disturbs me. The two strongest forces in her life are on collision course. I do not think that there is anything to be done. On the other hand, I can think of no one to talk to except you.

Suppose I had not paid the sister's way home, but let her drift off into the mountains, or down to Memphis? Would it have made a difference? Would it at least have postponed the collision? I haven't the remotest; but I do have an eerie feeling as of having shot an arrow in the air.

The touch of evening contains a touch of autumn. The fields of wheat have all been cut, and frost could come at any time, so unpredictable are first frosts in this land of fluctuations. It does make a person angry, that the first frost, coming almost at the height of summer, should kill all the petunias, and then there should follow many a balmy day on which they might be enjoying themselves like crazy.

I hope that you are well, and that I will hear from you soon, to the effect that my forebodings are but old things recollected in stolidity and lethargy.

67. Mr. Brown to Miss Gray

Autumn has come, by the calendar, though the lotuses, happily steaming down there, do not show it; and I think it may be time to go home. That you should hear from me after so many weeks of longing for a letter is confirmation of the old adage: news is bad news.

Let us now see to the blooming of the hundred flowers whose seeds were planted in my first paragraph.

On this first day of autumn (by the calendar) I had for the first time a telephone call from Mr. Shiraito, the father of our Miss Shiraito. It was extremely polite. I answered the telephone myself, as I always do. He said that he wished to speak to my secretary in a matter too trivial to be a demand upon my valuable time. I said that I preferred when possible to be without secretarial assistance. He wondered, then, if he might impose upon my busy schedule in a matter in which the use of the telephone would be a rudeness.

So we met this evening at a most exceedingly elegant place in Ginza, one of those places that charge at about the rate of a corporation lawyer or a heart surgeon, and let you know that this is the case, if you receive the signals properly, by the accoutrement of their functionaries and menials. One who thinks it time to depart this land enjoys being taken to such a place, at commencement of autumn; for with it comes recall of many things, and an instilling of ambitions. Who knows, if one works hard and forms the right connections, one might, eventually, return with enough prestige to make reservations at such a place, and enough money to pay the bill.

There were profuse apologies. My fame, he said, had reached even unto his narrow, constricted, shadowed corner of the realm; and the benevolent wisdom which I had distributed so generously, at such an expenditure of priceless hours, over all those channels, had led him to wonder whether, in a most insignificant regard, he might avail himself of a tiny part of it.

What he wished to know was whether I had information as to the whereabouts of his second daughter.

None at all for some days, said I. Why did he ask?

His second son and second daughter, he said, had vanished from sight. The latter had left a note saying that they hoped to do something in another realm. The former had sent a note, to that same effect, to his grandmother in Sendai.

I told him of our last meeting, towards the end of last month. I did not as a matter of fact remember when exactly it was, but reference to an almanac makes me sure that it was two or three nights before the end of the month. She made such a thing of the moon, and the fact that only true lovers of the moon would be up at such an hour viewing it.

I did not tell him of the moon, for it would have made him guess the lateness of the hour, but I did tell of a curious happening which suggests tension. She took up a great vat of lotuses, a gift from an earlier visit, and threatened to drop it on a passing policeman. I had to wrest it from her arms.

I think I am now brought to the matter of my proposed departure. I am tired of having irrelevancies drawn from me, on this and that channel, by interviewers who are devilishly clever at avoiding relevancies. When last I was interviewed by Miss Blacktarn, I found myself wishing that I had a watergun, with which to close those big black tarns of eyes.

Another thing is happening. Very few people come this way. So many things are the result of calculation, and the bottom line reveals to more and more people, I think, that I am not worth much. My energies are expended upon unproductive matters like channels, and I have caused embarrassment, and could do it again.

So the time has probably come to leave. I have almost decided to accept one of those scholarships for reporters who have been away and want to familiarize themselves once more with their native land and all its wrathful grapes. I have had a good time. I think that the chances of having another will be improved if I have a time of absence.

I agree with you about Mr. Shiraito. He is an estimable man.

"It is nothing to worry about, really," he said, turning to play pattycake-pattycake with a professional entertainress of *most* extreme elegance.

"If they set up housekeeping somewhere, it will not be the worst possible solution," he said, the game of pattycake-pattycake finished, and the lady, as they always are, the victor. "As for more drastic and final solutions, I do not think that either of them is the type."

Which accords reasonably well with my own views. I wanted to ask what effect this happening would have on plans for the youngest daughter, but did not. I have not met her or the brother. I think that our Miss Shiraito will be back, one day.

In which condition you may expect me soon. If I tell you that I will be arriving by bus, on a day when the mountains are golden with the *populus tremuloides* of autumn, will you come and meet me?